THE CASE OF THE MISSING HAND

by
Jon Edmiston

Grosvenor House
Publishing Limited

The right of Jon Edmiston to be identified as the author of this
work has been asserted in accordance with Section 78
of the Copyright, Designs and Patents Act 1988

The book cover is copyright to Jon Edmiston

This book is published by
Grosvenor House Publishing Ltd
Link House
140 The Broadway, Tolworth, Surrey, KT6 7HT.
www.grosvenorhousepublishing.co.uk

This book is a work of fiction. Any resemblance to
people or events, past or present, is purely coincidental.

A CIP record for this book
is available from the British Library

ISBN 978-1-83975-300-8

Prologue

Lady Pottersby was a recluse, she wanted to keep her acquaintances to as few as possible and she never allowed people in her house unless they were working or had a reason to be there but when one of her guests is found murdered with their hand missing, she must finally turn to someone she neither knows nor trusts, a builder working in her house whose only experience of detective work was on a murder mystery weekend. Can Ruff solve the case of the missing hand or will Lady Pottersby be the killers next victim ?

Preface

Hello reader, My name is Jon Edmiston and I am the author for this book. This book was a result of myself watching detective stories. I have always had a fascination for murder, not the real thing just what you read in books like this one and what you see in films. What brought this book into being for me was Miss Marple. I am someone who loves the old things not so much the new and my favourite detectives are Miss Marple, Taggart and of course Cracker and they are all unique in their own way, Taggart being the late great Mark McManus. It was however Miss Marple who brought this book about. To me there is and will only ever be one Miss Marple, the fantastic Joan Hickson, the way she portrayed the character was in my opinion second to none and when she sadly passed, they should have stopped the series as you cannot replace someone like that.

Ruff is like Miss Marple in that he is as an unlikely a detective as you could ever hope to meet and this is how Ruff came about. When you think of detectives, you think of some intelligent college professor or someone from CID, not a little old lady from a quaint English village, I mean how would she cope if the baddies decided to cut up rough. With my character there are parallels to Miss Marple as he too is as unlikely a detective maybe even more so than Miss Marple, unlike Miss Marple he has the strength but whereas Miss Marple knew what she was doing Ruff was thrust into the situation by a terrified old lady. I do not want to spoil the book by giving away the plot but unlike my first book, this does have a technical side to it which makes you think.

Finally, I also tried to inject humour into it, I like simple straight forward comedy that does not need to be explained, the sort of comedy where when it happens you know it's funny and you are not left thinking should I have laughed there.

That's about it, I did enjoy putting this together and I hope you enjoy reading it.

Introduction

My name is Jon Edmiston, and this is a story about a dream I had. It was a vivid dream about a planet many millions of miles away, a planet called Sporg in a place called Moontown. Sporg is a planet the same as earth, same people, same hopes, same dreams, same problems, same murders, this is about one of them.

Part One

The Case of the Missing Hand

This took place at a mansion belonging to Lady Pottersby. Lady Pottersby was an elderly lady in her eighties, although she never let people know how old she was, people close to her knew. She was a very refined lady who enjoyed a simple life and kept herself to herself; although she was a millionaire and could afford the finer things in life, she chose to only have the bare minimum of help. She had a maid and a butler, the butler prepared her tea and helped her get to bed although she did have a stairlift, he helped her get into her night attire. Lady Pottersby lived in a large mansion on her own with over 60 rooms. Many people asked her, why do you live there, with your money you could buy a small cottage? But Lady Pottersby was a lady who became very attached to places, she had been born in the mansion and she intended to die there. She was an only child whose parents died when she was younger, she would have only been in her early twenties when her parents died. Her mother was a titled lady who was related to the royal family of Sporg. Sporg had a royal family who ruled the entire planet, her father had worked in the mines and died from emphysema as a result of sucking in many of the filthy materials in the mine; there was an enquiry but no one was ever found guilty. Sometimes she thought to herself, if it had been her mother, there would have been a more thorough investigation than the one that happened. Her mother was a wonderful doting person who always had time for her, she loved her mother and never forgot her; she always considered her special as many members of the royal family had children which they simply palmed out to the help, she was one of the lucky ones she kept telling herself. Despite outward appearances, Lady Pottersby was a lonely woman although she would never let anyone know this, sometimes she would spend hours alone in one of the many rooms in the mansion looking at her mother's photo and stroking it.

The mansion was quite old, and at the moment one of the wings was having major repair work done, again she could have had a team of workers in to speed up the process but she asked for only one; the man agreed on the understanding there would be no pressure on a time limit. One day, Lady Pottersby was in bed, it was just a normal day but as Lady Pottersby woke up, she could feel an unnatural chill crawl across her body causing her to flick open one of her eyes toward the window just to see a rivulet of water sliding down the glass. As Lady Pottersby was waking, she could hear footsteps a long way down the corridor, but they were getting closer. As the sound got closer, she heard a turn then a click as the magnificent marble door opened up, revealing Jarvis the butler. Jarvis was a tall man at over six foot, he had distinguished features and walked with purpose, he was dressed in a crisp white shirt with a butler's jacket thrust over his shoulders. He wore a pair of black shoes, which were very big and always announced him as he walked in the room as he always took care to make sure they were shining – not just shining, if you looked into them you would be blinded with the shine. Lady Pottersby often thought, how does he shine them and indeed with what? Jarvis was walking toward her with a silver tray containing a yellow flower and her breakfast, some lightly buttered toast and a hard-boiled egg. Also on the plate was a cup and a pot containing hot water, she always made a point of wanting her cup of tea done in her presence so she could see the teabag disappear. "Are we ready, m'lady?" announced Jarvis.

Lady Pottersby drew herself up as Jarvis waited patiently at the side of the bed. "Ready for what, Jarvis?" she asked.

He examined her face to see if she was serious or joking. A short glance revealed she was indeed joking. "For whatever today throws at us, m'lady."

"How is the weather today Jarvis?" she enquired.

"It is, indeed, quite inclement, m'lady," he replied. Even though Jarvis had been with Lady Pottersby more years than he cared to remember, she would not allow familiarity to creep in, even though she knew that Jarvis would lay down his life for her. Indeed it was not so long ago when the two went into town and she was accosted by a beggar, which caused him to put himself in her way, again the lady gave as good as she got, waving her umbrella viciously when asked for 10 pence for a cup of tea. Indeed, if Jarvis had not been so quick on his feet, he may well have been the victim of a castration by the metal spike poking out the end.

"Are you there, Jarvis?" she called.

He lifted his head to look at her. "Reminiscing, m'lady," he replied.

She shot him a kindly glance before speaking. "We have been through many adventures, haven't we, Jarvis?" she said.

"Hopefully, many more to come, m'lady," he replied. Jarvis headed to the door leaving the lady with her breakfast.

Lady Pottersby had a bell to ring, actually it was more of a cord, one quick pull and Jarvis would come running, although to be fair he was always there or thereabouts. Lady Pottersby looked around her huge bedroom, there was a huge crystal chandelier above her and a private bathroom almost as big as the room itself. Inside the bathroom was a toilet and a cold marble floor, the mirror was encased in a gold frame, and the bath was also encased around the edges in gold with gold taps. Although the staff amounted to two, apart from the builder who was only temporary, no one would have ever been able to find any dust around the mansion and this she was proud of. As time rolled on, Lady Pottersby ate through her toast and brutally assaulted her boiled egg with all the strength she could muster. When she finished, she again cast a glance to the window, but if anything, the rain was lashing down worse than ever.

Lady Pottersby now turned her attention to her newspaper as she started to peruse the headlines. *Death and destruction,* she thought, *is that it? Political correctness is all well and good, but death and destruction still haven't been wiped out.* Lady Pottersby was born in the late thirties when people had a sense of humour and things were not taken so deadly serious, she put down the paper and let out a sigh. *I wish something exciting would happen,* she thought but little did she know, soon she would get her wish. Downstairs in one of the other 60 rooms, the maid was cleaning; she was well paid, and to be fair, there was not a great deal of work to be done as no one else lived in the mansion. The maid was called Sarah, she was about five foot six with long blond hair, she wore a Victorian maid's outfit which did not do anything for her figure, but it was probably the way it was designed she thought. She was in her mid-twenties with a perfect figure; she was not too fat and not too thin, but she was not interested in relationships. She remembered what her parents said, career first, reproduction and relationships later. *Relationships,* she thought as she flicked around her duster. Back upstairs, Lady Pottersby was getting ready to be up for the day, although all she did was sit in her chair looking out onto her huge garden. It was still her life, she thought, and she was determined to enjoy it no matter how long she had left. Although Lady Pottersby preferred her own company, she had many friends, and a lot of them were royalty due to her mother's connections. Many times, she was invited to the royal palace, but she declined as she simply was not that kind of person. But today, she thought, she was going to push the boat out, today was the day of Lady Pottersby Garden Party Queen. This was a garden party no one would ever forget, she thought, she had the space, the help and the connections, so why not? She was convinced her butler and the maid could do it all, although they probably would disagree.

Sarah was coming to the end of her shift, she had cleaned most of the ornaments and she was ready to go home and put her feet up, but she had one last thing, the cellar; it was a huge cellar and a huge job so she needed some kind of sustenance before she could continue. Sarah remembered what Lady Pottersby said once, treat my home like yours, make drinks, watch television just please don't steal from me. It was not that Lady Pottersby did not trust Sarah, it was just, to be honest, that the house was so huge if someone did steal something you would never know. Fortunately for Lady Pottersby, Sarah was a very honest girl. Sarah headed to the fridge, knowing there would be a cold drink for her in the huge fridge. Like everything in the house, the fridge was not your standard fridge, it was nearly as big as the bathroom, there was a reason for this, Lady Pottersby had a fear of running out of food, she also thought, if she had a party, the food was already there. Sarah headed for the fridge and opened it, she walked inside and found Jarvis already there examining the food. "Hello, Jarvis, midnight snack?" she quipped.

Jarvis turned around and looked at her with friendly eyes, but even so, Sarah could see trouble living behind his pupils. "What is it, what's wrong?" she blurted out.

"Lady Pottersby is desirous of holding a party," said Jarvis.

"How is that a problem?" asked Sarah.

"Five hundred guests, me and you to prepare the tables and the party," he said.

"Just us!" she blurted. "How?"

Jarvis looked towards her then back toward the fridge before unhooking a slab of meat off the hook. Jarvis threw the meat over his shoulder. "I don't know but we have got to try," he said.

Sarah looked at Jarvis as she tried to help him secure the slab of meat on his shoulder. "Why doesn't she just get more staff in?" she asked. Jarvis looked toward her as he headed out the fridge, grabbing the door and swinging it shut. "Wait, I wanted a—"

Jarvis put his free hand in his pocket and threw out a can. "Drink," he finished.

"How did you know?" she asked.

"You always want a drink about this time," he returned. She pulled back the ring pull, taking a drink before laughing.

Upstairs Lady Pottersby sat on her chair looking out the window at the raindrops chasing each other down the pane. After a while, the door opened, and Sarah stepped in. "Ma'am," she said.

"Yes, Sarah," she replied.

"About this garden party. Do you not think that perhaps you could hire outside help? It is a bit much for me and Jarvis," she said.

"Jarvis assured me that you could manage it," she answered.

Sarah was trying to think what to say before quickly looking toward the window. "What if the rain does not let up?" said Sarah, thinking this would make her rethink.

"It's an indoor party, it's being held in the ballroom, we are having stalls, food and games, please don't let me down," she asked. Sarah was about to argue again, but then she looked into her eyes and could see she was starting to look sad.

"Ma am," she said as she did a curtsy and then backed out of the room. Sarah and Jarvis started to work on getting the garden party ready for the guests, but before long, help was to arrive in the form of the stallholders. All of a sudden, the ballroom had been transformed into the biggest garden party Moontown had ever seen.

"Jarvis, Sarah, you've outdone yourselves, well done." She handed the two a pair of small envelopes containing hundreds of notes. "For your trouble," she said. Sarah started to turn red as she became embarrassed, after all she had said, how she had hundreds of notes in her hands. *Fair's fair*, thought Sarah, *she can afford it, but it's the thought that counts.* Quick as a flash, she took the money and put it into her pocket as did Jarvis. As time passed, the ballroom started to fill with a throng of voices, some high and some low, people from all walks of life either standing behind stalls or buying something from them.

As Sarah walked around, she came across a stall owned by a Charles Canterbury, Sarah looked around to see what he was selling, she could not quite make out what he had, but it all looked very expensive. "You like what you see, my dear?" a voice boomed out. Sarah looked up at the owner of the voice, and she had to stop herself from laughing; looking at him, he resembled a badger. He was about five foot six with grey bushy eyebrows and a sharp pinstripe suit in yellow. His trousers had razor-sharp creases which looked as though maybe they could do damage as they were so sharp, back to his face he had a bushy grey beard which looked as though it lived in his mouth, every time he spoke it seemed to vanish into his throat.

"I, er, just wondered what you were selling, sir," said Sarah desperately trying to stifle a laugh.

"Charles, me dear," came back the voice, "I have a wide variety of things I didn't really need, just kicking round the house," he finished. Again, Sarah examined the table, anything to take her away from his face. On the table was laid out glittery gold jewellery and something that looked like a Fabergé egg, next to it was a jewel-encrusted snuff box, she picked it up and examined it. It was small and silver, emitting a strange smell, but it was the jewellery that held her attention. "That, my dear, is a snuff box; five hundred buttons," he announced.

Five hundred, she thought, *five hundred for something I don't want in the first place*. "No, I'm sorry, I'm just browsing," she told him.

Once again, she picked up the egg. "That's a Moontown egg, similar to Fabergé but much more expensive and far more rare; two million buttons," he said.

Sarah almost fainted, she had never seen two million, she wasn't sure such a number even existed. "Anything cheap that a maid could afford?" she asked.

Charles looked like he was about to explode, his face became red and he was making puffing noises. Just as he was about to launch a verbal assault on her, a voice rang out, "Sarah, can you help hand out the food?" said Lady Pottersby.

Charles's face came down and regained its normal colour and shape. "Oh, you are Pottersby's maid, are you?" he asked.

"Yes," she came back.

Charles fumbled on the table, then as if he remembered something, he shoved his hand down and began to scribble before bringing up a black and white photo. "There you go, my dear." He handed her a photo of himself in his army uniform, signed Field Marshal.

Sarah placed it in her pocket, thanking him, she then walked toward Lady Pottersby. "Where are you going?" she asked.

"To get the sandwiches," she replied.

"No," she said, "I was saving you from yourself, the field marshal is a nice man, but unless you are a multi-millionaire, I doubt you can afford anything of his. Sometimes, I think he does it to show off."

"Why bring all those things to a garden party?" asked Sarah.

"Tell me, Sarah, have you ever been to a garden party?" asked Lady Pottersby.

"Yes, but not like this," she replied.

"The idea of a garden party is to eat food and to talk to friends, make friends, but occasionally we have other things, stalls, tombola, but this one is a high-class party. Feel free to help yourself to food, but I'd avoid the stalls unless you have hidden millions I know nothing about," she said.

Sarah walked away, feeling a little sad but more educated about the lives of the upper classes. As she slouched away, she was spotted by Jarvis. "Don't feel so bad, Sarah, there are some movie stars that would not be able to afford what he's selling or indeed any of them." Jarvis put his arm around Sarah as the two retired to the kitchen to start on the sandwiches left for them.

Lady Pottersby wandered around her large ballroom examining all the tables when she saw out of the corner of her eye a lady in a blue suit that looked kind of out of place at a garden party. "I, say, Lady Pottersby," said the voice. She quickly changed direction and quickly headed toward the table as, after all, she was the hostess and she did not want to appear rude. She quickly arrived at the table. "Lady Pottersby," announced the lady as she extended her body over the table to plant a kiss on her cheek. "Do you not remember me?" she enquired.

For a moment, Lady Pottersby looked embarrassed, then she had to give in. "I'm so sorry, I don't," she stammered.

"Lady Margaret Rudge," she announced.

Lady Pottersby's expression altered as though a light had gone on in her head. "We were at school together, weren't we?" she said.

"Yes, in class together for six years but to be fair, it has been a long time," Rudge added. Lady Pottersby got herself and her friend a drink and sat down at her table and began to reminisce about the past.

Jarvis the butler was carrying out his duties when he realised that he was running out of champagne. Where was Sarah? he wondered. Jarvis started to look for Sarah and eventually she appeared. "Ah, Sarah, can you get me some more champagne from the cellar, please," said Jarvis.

"I'll need help," asked Sarah, Jarvis looked at her. "It's heavy," she said.

Jarvis walked over to the field marshal. "Excuse me, sir, me and Sarah are going to get some bottles from the cellar, could I ask you to look after the party, please?" said Jarvis.

"No, problem, my good man, be delighted to, get me out from behind this desk, what," he announced.

Suddenly without warning a scream rang out, tearing the air like the crack of a whip. Jarvis bolted to the door with the field marshal following as close behind as his fitness would allow. When Jarvis and the marshal arrived, Sarah was openly sobbing, with the building worker comforting her. "Excuse me, sir, what are you doing to Sarah?" he asked indignantly.

"In there, my son," replied the building worker, "be warned it's messy, love." Jarvis entered the room with the field marshal to find a body propped against the wall with its hand cut off and blood pumping out. Jarvis openly vomited on the floor, but the field marshal seemed unperturbed. "How come you're not vomiting?" asked the building worker.

"I was in the war, I've seen far worse than that," he said.

Finally, Lady Pottersby turned up. "What is going on in here?" she said.

"Dead body, love," said the building worker, at which point, Lady Pottersby collapsed.

Part Two

Whodunnit

Lady Pottersby started to cough. As she became more aware of her surroundings, she could see a face staring at her and a voice in her head, "She is coming around."

"Oh, my word, what happened?" enquired Lady Pottersby with an air of exasperation in her voice.

"You passed out, love," said the man.

"Who might you be?" she asked the scruffy-looking person.

"Ruff rs," he said.

"Ruff rs," she replied.

"Yes, m'lady," he answered.

"Ruff rs, what sort of a name is that to give someone?" she said.

"I was adopted, love, abandoned by my parents when I was a child, I never knew them. The orphanage was real rough and I never liked any of the names they gave me. When I left, I did various schemes to see what sort of career I could do, and someone suggested I tried building work. I tried me hand at building work and what do you know? Anyway, one day I was working on a building site and I think me crack was showing," he said in his rough voice. At this point, Lady Pottersby shuddered imagining the image. "Someone shouted, 'look, it's a rough-arse building worker,' I kind of liked the name, so I kept it."

"I don't think, I like my employees having such names," she replied.

"Well, missus, technically I don't work for you," he replied.

"While you work on my property, you are my employee," she said.

Lady Pottersby turned back to Jarvis. "Well, what do you suggest?"

"The police, ma'am, the detectives must be informed," he replied.

"Must they," she strained, "you know how I feel about people coming into my house, is there no other way?"

Jarvis looked at his mistress. "I'm afraid not," he said with an air of defeat on his lips. The room fell silent for a moment as though everyone was quietly thinking their own thoughts, when suddenly.

"Wait, has anyone here any experience of detective work," she pleaded. Her eyes scanned the room in desperation, hoping that perhaps someone would jump at the opportunity to become famous.

It seemed like an eternity but at last someone spoke, "I'll have a crack if you fancy, love, I've always wanted a go," said Ruff rs.

Jarvis was quick to respond, "I really don't think we can—"

Lady Pottersby cut him off halfway, "Yes, but do you have experience?" she asked in desperation.

The answer was slow in coming but finally did arrive, "I went on a murder mystery weekend and I got a prize." A big release of air escaped the room as there was a collective sigh, apart from Lady Pottersby who looked strangely impressed.

"You have sold me. Do what you have to, Ruff, and I'll pay any expenses you need to carry out your investigation," she announced.

"What about your house?" he asked.

"Once it's over, you can get back to your real job, Ruff, now get to work on this," she said as she headed out the room.

Ruff stood up straight and proud like a peacock just after revealing its feathers as he held his overalls in pride. Ruff was an honest, down to earth man who had leapt from job to job and let opportunity slip through his fingers, but finally he had found something and this time, the outcome would be different he promised himself. "Detective Ruff rs," he announced to himself. He was 56 years old and a shortish man no more than 5 foot 4, he wore blue overalls and silver glasses. Ruff also had a beard encasing his chin with whiskers, it looked to anyone who saw Ruff that he must dye his hair as everywhere on his body was grey apart from the hair on his head.

Just then the door opened and Lady Pottersby spoke, "Ruff, go upstairs and find a suit, there will be one on the top floor in the cupboard hanging up. If you're going to be my detective, we need you to look the part." Ruff headed out the door and down the corridor, which was littered by every artist you could think of, she was either an art collector or kleptomaniac. Finally, he reached the grand staircase, which was adorned by a gold railing which hugged the stairs like a giant snake. Grabbing hold, Ruff proceeded to walk upstairs to the room at the top. In the room at the top of the stairs, there were many suits hanging up. Ruff looked at them and decided which one he would wear. It was difficult; he thought should he wear something smart or should he wear something that made him look like a detective. Ruff put his hand into the wardrobe and picked out a suit that he thought would look good on him. The suit was all blue; it looked from a distance as though it was pinstripes. Ruff thought for a moment, was this the correct suit to wear or would he be better wearing a black suit and looking smarter? Ruff pondered his options, then he finally decided on the black suit as he felt it would make him look more like a detective. After choosing his suit. Ruff descended the stairs and went back to join the others, ready to begin his adventure as a detective.

Back with Lady Pottersby, Jarvis said, "Do you think this is a good idea making an amateur a detective? Do you not think it would be a better idea to get the police?"

Lady Pottersby looked at her faithful friend and said as diplomatically as possible, "We can assist, you know I have connections to the royal family, we can give Ruff all the help he needs. With my guests, there cannot be more than 100 people in this building, no one is leaving until this mess is sorted out," she replied.

"M'lady, we have but 60 bedrooms and most are unmade beds; considering the shock Sarah has just had finding the body, I do not think either her or myself are in any kind of position to make the beds for 60 guests."

Lady Pottersby thought for a moment. "I have an idea. Ruff can talk to all of them, and when he is satisfied, he can let them go. After all, we know where they all live anyway," she said.

"Yes, m'lady," said Jarvis with some exasperation.

Just then, Ruff appeared and joined the two of them standing in the corridor. "Right then, I'll need to see the body, love," he boomed.

Jarvis and Ruff headed back to the body, which had been covered by a sheet. Ruff pulled back the sheet and began to examine the body. After about five minutes, Jarvis broke the silence, "Do you see anything, sir?"

"Well, I'd say female, about mid-thirties with dyed blond hair, you can see the dark roots," he said.

"The cause of death, sir, I suppose blood loss with the missing limb," he said with some degree of authority.

His cocky smile soon vanished as Ruff gave him the news. "No," he said.

"No?" came back Jarvis.

Ruff invited Jarvis to kneel before the body as he gently ran a finger across the lips, removing his finger he showed it to Jarvis. "That is some sort of drug," he said.

"So that was it?" said Jarvis.

Ruff moved the blond hair away and gently lifted the neck. "Or this," he said.

Jarvis almost vomited as he saw a deep ligature wound across the throat of the dead woman. "So, it has to be this," said Jarvis.

"I would say, one or the other, it's just I need to find out which was the first thing administered," he said.

"Do you know any chemistry?" asked Jarvis curiously.

"No, we just collect a sample and send it to a lab for forensics," said Ruff as he removed the sample from her lips and gently placed it in a tube.

At that point, Jarvis pulled Ruff to the side. "You know why you have this job, don't you?" said Jarvis. "Her ladyship wants no one from the outside in." At that point, Ruff handed the tube to Jarvis.

"You analyse it," said Ruff as he removed his gloves and walked away.

Lady Pottersby was talking to her guests when Jarvis appeared. "Excuse me, m'lady," he said.

"Excuse me," said Lady Pottersby as she turned from her guest to focus her attention on the butler. "Yes, Jarvis."

"Ruff has found a sample, and he wants it analysed, but I explained how you do not want outsiders coming in."

He handed the glass tube to Lady Pottersby. "What's the powder?" she asked.

"That is what Ruff wanted to know," said Jarvis.

"Leave it with me, I should have the results in a couple of hours, I know a private chemist."

Sarah was busy cleaning with her duster when Ruff approached her from behind. "Hello, Sarah," he said.

"Hello, Ruff," she replied.

"Lady Pottersby gave me permission to interview everyone I saw fit."

"You think they did it, Ruff?" asked Sarah.

"One of them, certainly," said Ruff, "which one is a bit more tricky."

Sarah took Ruff to one side. "What you may find even more tricky, is the fact that none of them will talk to you. You ever heard the expression, silver spoon in their mouth?" said Sarah.

"Of course," said Ruff.

"With this lot, it slid down their throats and blocked their vocal cords, none of them will talk," said Sarah.

"None of them," replied Ruff.

"There is maybe one, this one here." Sarah took Ruff over to an elderly yet quite distinguished-looking gentleman with medals adorning his chest which were shimmering in the light.

Ruff extended his hand. "Good afternoon, sir, I am Ruff. I was hired by Lady Pottersby to discover the identity of the murderer. Do you mind answering a few questions?" said Ruff.

"Fire away, Ruff," said the man.

"Could you tell me your name please?" asked Ruff.

"Buttocks, sir, Barrington Buttocks," he said with a loud booming voice.

All of a sudden, the air was torn apart by laughter. "I'm sorry, what?" repeated Ruff.

"Buttocks, sir, Colonel Barrington Buttocks." Again the laughter tore across the room like a fighter plane's engine, slicing the air.

"What is so damn funny, is it my name?" he enquired.

Ruff was trying to compose himself as Sarah had already gone and was in hysterics on the floor. "Sarah, perhaps you had better go, I can handle this, me and Colonel B, Colonel Barrington." Ruff stopped himself from laughing. Sarah flew out of the room, trying desperately to hold in a laugh that was bursting to come to the surface.

"If you want help from me, you had damn well better behave, you young scallywag. I'll tell you this, none of the others will talk, I am the only conversation you will have with anyone today."

"Why do you think that, sir?" Ruff asked.

"It's not what I think, sir, it is what I know. None of us did this horrid thing and we see no need to defend ourselves, I am merely being courteous," said the colonel.

"Can you think why anyone would want to murder her?" asked Ruff.

"I appreciate, sir, that you have been given the unenviable task of getting the goods, shall we say, on one of us, but don't you think it would be wiser to find out who it is before you accuse anyone or indeed suppose a motive," said the colonel.

"Of course, and you're right, I apologise, Mr Buttocks."

"Colonel Buttocks, I was in the war, you know. Maybe when you discover the identity, you could talk to Bertha?"

"Bertha?" said Ruff.

"Bertha Breasts," said the colonel.

"Bertha B; you have got to be kidding me," he said under his breath.

The five hours had now passed, and the mystery was about to be revealed as, at long last, the lab results came back. "Well?" said Lady Pottersby as Ruff examined the results.

"It's as I suspected, love, it was a muscle relaxant," said Ruff.

"I don't understand," said Lady Pottersby.

"The hand was removed to make us think she died of loss of blood, then the strangulation mark was not meant to be seen but we saw it; what we were not meant to find was the chemical on her lips. She was drugged, then when she was relaxed and willing to do anything and unable to feel anything, she was strangled. The hand was removed to make us think she bled to death," said Ruff.

"So, who killed her?" asked Lady Pottersby.

"I have two theories: someone old, the drug was to make her easier to strangle so she would not put up a fight or my second theory is that the person was scared, and they used the relaxant so they had time to kill her knowing no one would come running if they heard a noise, which they wouldn't because of the drug," said Ruff.

"So, we are looking for an elderly person with a grudge against the woman?" said Lady Pottersby.

"Not exactly," suggested Ruff.

"Pardon!" said Lady Pottersby.

"The removed hand was removed to distract us. Maybe it was a young, strong person and the rest was just a distraction, maybe an argument that went wrong and it was made to look like a murder. There are so many possibilities," said Ruff.

Lady Pottersby looked deeply perturbed. "So, you can't find who did it?" said Lady Pottersby.

"I think, maybe I can," said Ruff. "However, I need to know who she is; we need a post-mortem or at least an identification."

The entire house was called up one by one until they got to the final guest. "Yes, I know her, it's Evelyn Trubshaw. She works in the paper shop, but what anyone would have against her, I don't know," said the guest.

"Your name, please, miss," said Ruff.

"Barbara Lane," she said as she walked away.

Ruff headed back to see Lady Pottersby. She sat all alone in the drawing room, peering out the window at the world passing her by. As Ruff entered, he gazed around in awe at the splendour that surrounded him. Like the stairs and countless other rooms, this room was also covered with paintings, the only odd thing about this room was that someone appeared to have forgotten to put any furniture in it. Lady Pottersby sat in a small wooden chair perched against the window with a view to the outside, also in the room was a lone leather settee and a full-length mirror hanging against the far wall. The knock came quickly, and it brought life out of Lady Pottersby. "Enter," she said in a shrill voice.

The door opened to reveal Jarvis standing by the door. "Begging your pardon, m'lady, but Ruff is here to see you."

"Send him in," she said. Ruff appeared and walked over to Lady Pottersby as the door closed behind him. "Ah, my dear fellow," she announced.

"Ay up, love," he said in his broad accent.

"Well, what have you found out?" she asked.

"Well, apparently, the girl used to work at a paper shop," said Ruff.

"Not Evelyn?" pleaded Lady Pottersby.

"Yes, she's been identified by one of her friends or leastways someone who knew her, all we have to do now is find out why."

"You have my permission to contact all my house guests and speak to them to find out what they know."

"I know one thing, someone downstairs murdered her, we just don't why," said Ruff.

The day was starting to draw to a close and Ruff was pondering over a drink with Sarah about what had happened downstairs. Ruff sat at the kitchen table looking around, normally only the catering staff were allowed in here, but due to circumstances, Lady Pottersby had said that Ruff could have full access to all the house. The kitchen, like the other rooms, was huge. In the corner stood a huge oven with at least 10 different dials, for what he did not want to ask, Ruff thought to himself, the last time he had seen anything like this was at a crematorium. Next to the oven was a giant washing machine and again loads and loads of dials, probably unnecessary but nevertheless they were there. And, of course, no kitchen would be complete without tons and tons of cupboards and drawers holding spices and herbs and various culinary implements, and as a kitchen, it did not disappoint. Finally, the kitchen was finished off with a simple wooden table in the middle of the floor, which could have seated at least 15 people. But as Ruff knew, there was only Jarvis and Sarah on the staff and, as far as he was aware, Sarah was not allowed in here, except for now as this was a special occasion. Sarah sat down next to Ruff at the table and tried to follow his gaze. Ruff was looking at the myriad of knives hanging from hooks on the walls of the kitchen, there were knives for every occasion and each one razor-sharp. "Is that it, is that how he did it, Ruff?" she quizzed.

"Is that how who did it?" enquired Ruff.

"The killer," came back Sarah.

Ruff took a moment to digest what she had just said. "Hmm, oh no, I was just looking at the knives, I've never seen so many," said Ruff. "Sarah, do you mind if I ask something?" enquired Ruff.

"Certainly, Ruff, I am a virgin," she said as she opened her top, allowing her breasts to balloon over her bra. Ruff was quite taken aback as he stared at her. "Thanks for that, but could you put them away as that's not what I wanted to know." Sarah looked disappointed as she began to stuff her breasts back inside her bra, she struggled for a moment, and finally they had disappeared.

"What, Ruff?" asked Sarah.

"What do you know about Lady Pottersby?" asked Ruff as he began to drink his coffee.

"How do you mean, Ruff?" she enquired.

"I mean, why all this setup? She could have loads of servants, it's not like she can't afford it, but yet she chooses just to have two. It must be hard work for you and Jarvis," he asked.

"Me and Jarvis are hard workers, but Lady Pottersby is old and I guess she just likes close family with her, and I guess me and Jarvis are as close to family as she is ever going to have. I mean, let's face it, who would want to sleep said Sarah, Ruff cut her off.

"Yes, thank you, you have been helpful. Goodnight," said Ruff.

Ruff opened the door leaving Sarah alone in the kitchen as he pondered his next move. All of a sudden, there was a loud pop and the bulbs in the hall blew, covering him in darkness. Then the sound hit him, a sound like rats scurrying to their destination, then up ahead at the far end of the corridor a faint yellow glow pierced the darkness. *What the hell?* thought Ruff. Slowly but surely, he headed toward the light. As Ruff headed down the corridor, he became aware of a change in temperature and an eerie laughing slowly but faintly filling his ears. Was this deliberate? he thought.

As Ruff got further down the corridor, the light was starting to fade but a quick look showed nothing but dark covering what once was behind him. Then as Ruff got closer, he suddenly stopped and thought to himself, *Why am I headed here? What is the light?* Soon the thoughts were rampant in his mind like giant whirlpools cascading through his dreams. Again, something made him look behind, but now an eerie whistling had started, it wasn't a tune just a single slow and deliberate whistle. *This is messed up*, thought Ruff. Again, Ruff decided the only sensible thing was to head to the light as he started to wonder if perhaps there was someone following him. If it was, was it someone who did not like the way the investigation was going?

Again, Ruff looked at the light and he was indeed getting nearer, but he was starting to get wet as though someone was pouring something from above his head and he was starting to find it hard to walk as every step was like stepping in treacle. The pain then began as Ruff's legs soon were not his own and, without warning, he fell to the ground. This was not the end by any means as Ruff knew whatever the light was is where he was headed. Then once again, the temperature changed as it became hot, very hot, searing heat; Ruff was in pain and began to scream out and the heat was getting worse. Just when Ruff thought the end had arrived for him, he heard a piercing scream in the darkness; it sounded like Sarah, had she been murdered? Ruff continued using his strength to pull himself toward his goal as the water became more violent and it looked as if instead of burning, Ruff would drown. In normal circumstances, he would swim away, but these circumstances were far from normal.

Now the time had come to take evasive action as things became worse, he began to hear voices, *how you doing old boy, can't get up can you, never mind, be going to sleep soon won't you? So, you failed, never mind, better luck next life.* Then a bloodcurdling laugh seemed to mock his very existence.

Ruff knew there was one way out, he needed that light. Again, he looked up, but the corridor suddenly changed and became blue then red then green, then back to blackness, then without warning, it became white like snow. But still he could see nothing as the temperature dropped a lot, to the point that the wind started again, then the voices, *come on lad, get them bricks laid, you won't get paid today.* Then the tunnel went black as Ruff could feel it moving and the strength returned to his legs as, suddenly, he could stand and walk. Then, as he was upright, an almighty force fired him like a missile out of a catapult toward the yellow light. *Is this the end or the answer?* thought Ruff as he held his breath as he was plunged to the yellow light. The cold, hard stone floor of the kitchen embraced Ruff as he was lying with his face pressed hard against the tiles.

"You, OK, old boy?" asked the colonel.

Ruff looked up to see Colonel Buttocks standing there. "Buttocks," he said.

"I hope this is not more of your disrespectful behaviour," he snorted.

"No, sorry, can you help me stand?" he asked. The colonel grabbed his arm and pulled him full-force to his feet as Ruff stood there tired but alive. "Colonel, are there ghosts in this house?" asked Ruff.

"Ghosts, old boy, ghosts," he repeated, "have you been smoking funny things, I know its legal in some countries, but you can keep it from me."

"How do you mean?" asked Ruff regaining his composure.

"A grown man believing in ghosts?" he mocked. "Can't you people accept that when you're dead, you're dead. There is no voodoo or black magic, that's just in horror movies," he quipped.

"Colonel Buttocks, I've just been through a massive dark tunnel, I heard things, saw lights, heard screams. It had to be real, it had to be," Ruff said.

Suddenly and without warning, Lady Pottersby appeared. "Good morning, Ruff. Ready to tackle another day?" she said.

"I'm sorry," said Ruff.

"Find my killer, Ruff," said Lady Pottersby.

"Lady Pottersby, I've just had the most awful experience," said Ruff nervously.

"Really, what was that?" she asked.

He was just about to speak when the colonel cut him off. Constipation, it's his bowels, can't shift it, he's got a whole warehouse full up there. Got anything, Lady Pottersby?"

"Well, I may possibly have some prunes or some cascara, I'll see."

Lady Pottersby stretched herself up and opened the cupboard, releasing a plate that nearly smashed on his head. "Nothing there," she said. Finally, she walked around to the other side of the kitchen and opened a smaller cupboard to find all manner of equipment in there. "Ah, here we go, cascara, with prune juice, double strength, this will purge those wicked bowels," she said, shaking the bottle from side to side before confidently cracking the childproof lock on top to get to the goodness. "Now then, what does it say here, two lots for stubborn bowels." Out came a long spoon and the evil-looking liquid almost melted the end, one spoonful then another.

Lady Pottersby saw the look on Ruff's face as the liquid took effect. Ruff let out a huge ooh noise from his throat as the stuff began to do its worst. "Don't worry, dear, that stuff is great even for wardrobe bowels." Lady Pottersby put the medicine back and headed for the door. As she was about to leave, she turned. "Don't forget to tell me when it's worked, dear," said Lady Pottersby.

"Don't worry, love, you will be the first to know, I guarantee it," strained Ruff.

"Don't you mean I'll be the second to know, surely you will be the first," she said as she left the room.

"Oh, yeah, I hadn't thought of that," joked Ruff as a thunderous fart cracked the air with a sound like a lion-tamers whip.

"Just two things, Colonel, why?" asked Ruff through strangled tones.

"If you'd been caught smoking funny things, you would have been dismissed, old boy," said the colonel. "The second?"

"What are wardrobe bowels?" asked Ruff.

"Have you ever heard the expression it's like trying to sh—"

Ruff cut him off, "Yes, unfortunately, I have."

"The thing is, I really saw what I saw, dreaming or not. No drugs, I promise, word of honour," said Ruff.

"No, drugs," came back the colonel.

"None," he replied.

"Ah, the er, toilet is through there," said the colonel apologetically.

"Thank you," said Ruff as a thunderous roar filled the air. Ruff flung the door open and hammered home the bolt on the door as the cascara and prune juice did its worst.

Ruff sat on his bed surrounded by newspaper, silently praying that the pain would stop, and he could have a good rest. But just as it appeared, the pain had stopped, like a bad toothache, once again it surfaced. Finally, the pain subsided and Ruff could lie down. Ruff was not and never claimed to be the perfect man, but he had been given a task to do, and now he must see it through; that task was to find and unmask a killer, but who and why. So far all he had was a bunch of people with odd names and a possible motive but nothing tangible. What did he have? he wondered. The girl worked at the paper shop, someone in the house knew her, one person out of 100 interviewed. Was it significant that she had her hand removed, to stop identification or was it, as he suspected at first, perhaps a vain attempt to disguise the real cause of death, strangulation? And what about the muscle relaxant? Could it have been someone not physically capable of killing her but knowing that come hell or high water, she had to die as she knew a secret? This was too much, Ruff was a building worker, a brickie, a plasterer, a jack of all trades but not the trade of identifying killers of paper girls. Was it now time to say to Lady Pottersby, you can use the cascara on yourself and leave me alone, I quit?

Ruff lay back on his pillows as a million thoughts swirled in his head, such as where could he find something more vicious than cascara and slip it in the colonel's tea when he wasn't looking, that would teach the old bastard. Then another thought hit him, could there be another murder as this may have not been an isolated case. Ruff must have fallen asleep as when he woke it was dark and cold, he gingerly crept off his bed so as not to disturb his pain, but what time was it, he had no idea. He knew it was winter, so theoretically it could be early morning, but something in the back of his mind made him think that perhaps it was indeed the middle of the night. Ruff went to his door and opened it as he went to see if he could find clues. As he wandered around the mansion, it struck him how dimly lit it was for an old lady living on her own, this was indeed a dangerous situation he thought.

Ruff cupped his hands and was about to yell out when he realised, he still did not know the time, and if it was the middle of the night, the other members of the house would not appreciate him waking them up with uncouth noises that indeed did belong on a building site. Ruff continued to traverse the corridors, the mansion was large, and his sense of direction was non-existent but, somehow, he knew that he could find his way back to his bedroom. Suddenly, Ruff had a terrible pain in his stomach, it was indeed hunger, so again, struggling to find his way in the dark, he headed downstairs into the kitchen. As he finally got to the destination, he switched the light on and immediately became aware that all of the knives had disappeared. Was someone using them or was the killer off again? Ruff knew there was a huge freezer somewhere in this mansion but considering what had been happening over the past while, he felt it would be unwise to go into a walk-in freezer, instead he decided that he would try to make a sandwich. He filled the kettle with water and plugged it in waiting for the whistle, he somehow found the breadbin and a small knife as he began to slice some bread for sandwiches just as the kettle boiled.

Taking his sandwiches and tea to the table, Ruff sat down and began to think about what was going on. He knew someone in the house had murdered the girl, but if he wanted to prove it, he would need evidence. As time went on, Ruff became tired as his mind started to wander when he was awoken by one of the other guests. "Hello."

Ruff shot up from the table. "Hello," he said.

"Having a rest, are you?" said the person. He turned around to see a lady in a pink nightie with a very slim body with chestnut hair and a fresh face, which he thought was quite an achievement seeing as this must have been close to if not the middle of the night. Looking down her body, Ruff could make out she was wearing pink carpet slippers, so he could assume she had not been outside. "My name is Ruff, and yours?"

The lady looked at him, and a warm smile spread across her face. "Bertha Breasts."

Normally, Ruff would have been in hysterics but this night it was too late to start screaming with fits of laughter. "I see and how may I help you, Bertha?" said Ruff.

"I saw the light on downstairs and I came to see what was going on," said Bertha.

"I see," announced Ruff.

"Well, to be honest, I was also a bit worried, what with the murder, most of us had never experienced anything like this before."

"Most of you?" said Ruff.

"Well, a lot, like the colonel, were in the war so they have seen their fair share of death and destruction," she said.

Ruff thought carefully before engaging her in conversation, after all he knew someone in the house had done it, he just had to find out who. Bertha looked at Ruff with a sideways glance. "You don't trust me, do you?"

Again, Ruff looked at her. *What should I say?* he thought. "It's not that, it's just that someone in this house murdered that girl and if I tell you everything I know, it may mean that you have an advantage with information that I had not intended to give you."

Bertha looked at Ruff, wondering what to say. "You will need to talk to someone, or your information is going to be limited. I know what you are saying, but you have about 100 people to choose from, it's just as likely one of them committed the murder as me."

Ruff thought hard and then decided that what she was saying was indeed correct and he did need help. "OK, here is what I know. A girl has been murdered and from what I have been told she worked at the paper shop. What I am having trouble with is why on earth would someone want to do it? She was just a girl who worked in a paper shop, I can't imagine she threatened anyone," said Ruff.

"Maybe it wasn't her," said Bertha.

"How do you mean?" said Ruff.

"Maybe she knew something that she was not meant to, it could be just that simple," said Bertha.

Ruff thought, could it be that simple, that this poor, innocent girl had been murdered because she knew something she was not supposed to know? Let's be honest, he thought, murder has been committed for these reasons before. Ruff's brow furrowed as he thought hard. "I was thinking perhaps it was money motivated, but she is a girl who works at the paper shop, I would doubt she had much. Is Lady Pottersby rich?" asked Ruff.

"It's a good motive, I suppose, for murder but at the risk of depressing you, all of your suspects are upstairs in bed working hard on their alibis, and I would say nine out of ten will be false," said Bertha.

"What about you?" asked Ruff.

"Me?" asked Bertha.

"Yes, what's your alibi?" asked Ruff.

"I don't need one, feel free to arrest me, I won't resist, I know I have nothing to hide," said Bertha.

Strangely enough, thought Ruff, *I don't know her, but somehow, I know she is innocent*. His eyes slipped down to her protruding breasts. *At least of the crime, anyway*, thought Ruff.

"Is Lady Pottersby rich?" said Bertha. "I cannot say she is, but outward appearances suggest she is, the mansion, her demeanour," she concluded.

"Her demeanour?" repeated Ruff.

"Look at the way she presents herself, would you say this is how someone who struggles with money would dress?" asked Bertha.

Again, Ruff knew she was right. "So, who do you suggest I start my interviews with tomorrow?" asked Ruff.

"In my opinion, I would suggest Charles Clearwater, you will find him interesting but a bit self-opinionated," said Bertha.

Ruff shot a glance out of the window and could see the sun starting to break through as night gave way to day. "Tell me, do you think there will be another murder?" asked Ruff.

"Most murders are committed for a reason," said Bertha, "if the first one solved the problem the killer had, then I would say no, however if there are more threats to the killer, I'm sure there will be more." Bertha stood up and walked to the sink.

"Are you going?" asked Ruff.

"Need my sleep, don't I," said Bertha, as she finally left the room.

Now Ruff was alone in the room with his thoughts. How did this help? Was she really innocent, or was this simply to distract him? The one thing that mattered was, the next job was to interview Charles but that would have to wait until the morning.

The morning came far too quickly for Ruff. Placing himself down at the coffee table in the kitchen, he took out his pad and paper and began what he hoped would be a fruitful exercise.

Charles Clearwater walked into the room. He looked in his early twenties, he also had the appearance of a businessman but as he was warned, he also had an air of superiority about him. *Could this be the killer?* thought Ruff. Charles had a thin but fresh face with very pronounced cheekbones, he also was sporting a brown beard with tints of grey. He was dressed in a pair of white trousers and a neatly pressed shirt, which seemed out of place due to his position in society if indeed he was what he appeared to be.

"Are you Charles Clearwater?" asked Ruff.

Charles looked at him with disdain. "Do I need my solicitor? I am not sure I should even be talking to you. You're not a real detective, are you?"

Ruff decided the colonel was correct, this was not going to be easy trying to conduct interviews with these people. "Where were you on the night of the murder?" asked Ruff.

"I don't see my activities have anything to do with you, so if you don't mind, I have other things to attend to." Charles got up to leave, and a mammoth hand pushed him down.

"I think perhaps we should answer the questions the gentleman wants to know," said the voice.

Charles looked up to see Jarvis holding him down. "Well, really, sir," said Charles indignantly. Again, he attempted to raise up his body but to no avail. "OK, I'll tell you," he submitted.

"On the night of the murder, I was walking my dog Petals, I didn't hear or see anything," said Charles.

"About what time?" asked Ruff.

"I would say about 11pm and the walk lasted half an hour," he said.

Ruff looked concerned. "Eleven, isn't that a bit late?" he said.

Charles's voice shot up an octave or two as he did his best to appear posh. "I am fabulously wealthy and very well connected; my dog is a pedigree. Would you like me to spell that word? I should think you have never come across it before, have you? Although she is a very good dog, she has problems with her bowels, and she can only go at certain times." Ruff looked at Charles to make sure he was not lying. "If you don't believe me, phone the vet."

Ruff called over Jarvis. "When did the murder occur?" he whispered, so low that Charles never heard.

"Midnight, sir," said Jarvis.

"Sir?" said Ruff, very surprised.

"You are in her ladyship's employ and I have been requested to call you sir by powers beyond me, so sir I must call you."

Ruff turned back to Charles. "Can you think of anyone who would want to kill her ladyship or a reason perhaps?" said Ruff.

"That would be money I think; that's why all murders occur now, isn't it?" said Charles.

"I don't know, I'm not a murderer," said Ruff. "So, who might know more?" he asked.

"It's difficult, her ladyship employs so few people. I guess the main suspects are you or us," said Charles.

"That's stupid, I'm the detective, I'd hardly murder her," said Ruff.

"Try Maureen Beachwater, she has a grudge with just about anyone and she was missing on the night of the murders. If anyone knows anything about anyone in this house or on this planet, it's her."

Ruff started to scribble frantically on a piece of paper. "OK, you can go... for now." Charles got up and walked out the door. "Do you know Maureen Beachwater, Jarvis?" asked Ruff.

"Village gossip, sir, will say anything about anyone even if it's not true. Her husband is high in the Moontown council and is extremely wealthy, he has the top lawyers around, so if you try to take him on, be prepared for a rough ride," said Jarvis.

I think, I still need to talk to her, Jarvis" said Ruff.

"I shall get her, sir," said Jarvis. Ruff looked at his notes and shuffled them into the correct order as he attempted to be ready for his second interview. After a while, Jarvis came back in through the door. "She's gone, sir," said Jarvis.

"Gone where?" said Ruff.

That's the thing, nobody knows, one minute she's there and the next she has gone," said Jarvis.

"Well, it will have to be the next person, who is it?" said Ruff.

"Lucy Strain," said Jarvis.

"Do we have anything on her?" asked Ruff.

"Red hair, freckles, medium height, quite timid, will crack if pushed, but when cracked, her information becomes less than truthful," said Jarvis.

"How do you mean?" asked Ruff.

"She panics, she wants to be out the situation, so she tells you what she thinks you want to hear, irrespective of the consequences," said Jarvis.

"Sounds like a silly girl," said Ruff.

"Not silly sir, just worried," said Jarvis.

"Whatever; send her in," said Ruff with a hint of boredom in his voice.

Lucy sauntered into the room looking like she was headed for the electric chair, even Ruff saw it as concern rushed over his face. Maybe he now had the killer but still no proof. "Hello, Lucy. Now I will put some questions before you, they are not nice, but I feel you can answer them. So, where were you at midnight on the night of the murder, if you could tell us in your own words, please," said Ruff.

Lucy was in her late teens with red hair and ginger freckles, she stood about five foot nine, she was wearing a yellow dress as though she had just been doing painting. Lucy thought for a moment and finally broke her silence. "On the evening in question, I was baking biscuits, I do it quite often. I know her ladyship does not permit more than two, sometimes three, members of staff on her team, so I decided that they would be away if she came down."

"They?" asked Ruff.

"The biscuits," said Lucy.

"When I heard footsteps about five to midnight, I jumped, nearly scalding myself as I wanted it to look as though no one had been in. So, I gathered up my things and ran, next thing I know, I am heading back home with my cooking things," said Lucy.

Ruff looked very concerned and then turned to Jarvis. "Is she so bad?"

"I think she could be, sir," said Jarvis. Ruff turned back.

"Can you think why anyone would want to murder the paper shop girl?" said Ruff.

"Maybe it was the argument?" said Lucy.

"Argument?" repeated Ruff.

"At about five to midnight, I heard raised voices near her ladyship's bedroom, I was taking her up some of the biscuits I had made and as I got to her door, I heard arguing. It sounded like male and female, but the female voice did not sound like a woman it sounded like a girl, then on hearing this I left. I came back at about half past midnight to see if things had calmed down, and again I heard voices, but it sounded like male and female. I put my ear to the door to try to hear and I could not hear a lot, but something I made out was, *that girl will have to go*. I mean it could have been anyone but it's something I suppose," said Lucy.

"Thank you, Lucy, I may need you again," said Ruff. With that, Lucy got up and left. "Jarvis," called out Ruff.

"You called, sir," said Jarvis.

"I think we may have a lead. Lucy told me a lot, to be fair it was what she thought she heard, but if half of it is true, we could be closer to solving the mystery," said Ruff.

"I am glad to hear it, sir," said Jarvis.

The interviews stopped abruptly as Ruff felt he needed to try to piece together what he had before deciding which direction to go in next. Ruff got up from the table and headed down the corridor. As he got to the end of the corridor, he began the long walk up the staircase, as he was halfway up, a scream tore halfway through the building. Immediately he stopped and headed down in the direction of the freezer room to find Lucy standing shaking. "What's wrong, love?" asked Ruff. Lucy did not speak, only point. Ruff followed the direction of her finger to the half-open freezer door. It was wedged open by the body of Bertha Breasts; her body was hung up by three meat hooks, one through the back of her head and one each through her breasts, the killer had struck again.

Part Three

Murder Without Reason

As Jarvis entered the room, the sight greeting him caused him to vomit. As Jarvis recovered himself, Colonel Buttocks then entered not noticing the vomit and he slipped, landing on his back. "Well, really," he announced.

"I'm sorry, sir, but the sight of that lady. Why?" said Jarvis.

At this point, Ruff was in hysterics along with Lucy at the colonel's predicament. "I'm sorry, sir," announced Ruff.

"Yes, I am sure you are," said the colonel in a less than convincing tone.

"By gad, look at my jacket it's covered." The colonel started to stand up out of the pool of vomit when Lady Pottersby walked in opening the door, the door hit the colonel in the head sending him back down to the floor causing Ruff much more hilarity. "Damn your eyes, sir," announced the colonel as he slopped around in the vomit until, finally, he got up.

"I'm so sorry, Colonel, I did not see you there." Lady Pottersby looked at Ruff holding Lucy. "Whatever is the matter, my dear?" she announced as Ruff's gaze drew her to the freezer and Bertha's predicament, at which point she passed out.

Lady Pottersby awoke in her bed with a start. Had it all been a dream? It had to have been, two people dead, in her house, her home, no, why? Immediately she found the cord and pulled it down to summon Jarvis. It was not long before the sound of footsteps filled the air and the door was slowly opened. "Oh, Jarvis, tell me I have been dreaming, please," she begged.

"I'm sorry, ma'am, I cannot," he announced.

"So, what happened?" she asked.

"It looks as though Ruff was retiring for the evening when he heard a scream. He went to investigate to find Miss Bertha impaled by three hooks, two through each breast and one through her head," said Jarvis.

"I must see Ruff now," she announced.

"In here, ma'am, right now?" said Jarvis.

"Yes, its urgent," said Lady Pottersby.

Jarvis turned and left the room and headed down to find Ruff who was working on repairs to the mansion. "Her ladyship requests that you see her now," said Jarvis.

"Alright, love," said Ruff as he scratched his backside.

Up the stairs he went, entering the bedroom to find Lady Pottersby lying in bed looking worried. "Well, what news, are you any closer to finding the killer?" she asked.

Ruff looked at her with a knowing glance. "Well, I've got some ideas if you still want me," said Ruff.

"What on earth do you mean, of course I still want you," she spluttered.

"I just thought, with the second murder, it's starting to look like Cluedo, maybe you need professionals, love."

Lady Pottersby drew herself close to Ruff. "No outsiders, please, do this, protect me, and I'll pay you handsomely."

Ruff looked at her to see if she was indeed serious. "Well, if that's how you want it, love. What I've figured is, I don't think its money motivated as the girl from the paper shop had no money, even her parents didn't, so I reckon her murder was because she was in the wrong place at the wrong time. Bertha Breasts, that was brutal, three meat hooks, you did not need it, why? I would say Bertha was revenge for something; for what, I'm not sure."

"Have you interviewed all my guests?" she asked.

"No, love, I'd hardly started when I got stopped by the second murder," Ruff announced.

"Maybe you could interview some more guests" said Lady Pottersby

"Thing is, love, Bertha gave me some good leads but no names, maybe someone was listening in and that's what got her killed."

Ruff lifted himself off the sheets as Jarvis walked in with the breakfast. "Is there anything I can get to help you?" said Lady Pottersby.

"I'll have a bit of that egg if you don't mind, love," said Ruff as he pulled a piece of toast off the tray, dipping it in her egg before swallowing it. After eating the toast, Ruff left the room and headed back downstairs to the kitchen to start his interviews again.

"Jarvis, new egg and toast please," Lady Pottersby ordered.

"Yes, m'lady," said Jarvis.

"I don't know what to do now," said Ruff to himself as he stared down at the clues he had. With that, the door opened and in stepped Lucy.

"Hiya, Ruff, want to see my breasts?" she said playfully getting ready to remove her bra. "Not now, love, keep em under wraps till later, eh," said Ruff. Lucy looked disappointed as Ruff sat down. "Any ideas, my one lead has gone," said Ruff.

"Maybe go down the village, you could ask there, they would help. Who would know the murdered girl better than the employers?" said Lucy.

"It's a good idea, love, but I'm just a building worker, no one would talk to me," said Ruff.

"Use your title, tell them who you are and who you work for, I promise, they will talk to you," said Lucy.

Ruff looked at Lucy and then at the lack of clues on his paper. "Aye, love, maybe you're right." Ruff told Lady Pottersby where he was going and got on his bike, riding down to the village. The village of Moontown was very small, in fact it was like one of these small villages you read about that you could easily pass through without even knowing you had.

Eventually, Ruff arrived at his destination extricating his buttocks from the saddle first the left then the right as he chained up his bike, and began the walk to the paper shop, stomach hanging over his trousers with his builder's crack visible.

Ruff opened the paper shop door and the bell tinkled. Inside was your typical paper shop. To the left of the door was a chiller cabinet filled with drinks, and stands either side containing sweets and crisps, straight ahead was a stand with greetings cards for birthdays and the like. On another stand nearby were saucy holiday postcards, Ruff picked one up and chuckled as he read it. In front of him was a desk stretching from one wall to the other with a small hatch presumably for the owners to get behind so they could serve. On the floor, Ruff noticed a stack of newspapers still tied up with string in bundles. Glancing at the headlines of the *Moontown Gazette,* he could see the headline 'Lady Bertha Impaled', then later into the story they revealed her full name. Ruff chuckled as he thought of the headlines. Breasts impaled or something funnier he thought. As Ruff looked through all the items, a small man appeared; he was in his late sixties, going bald, and it looked like he was about to retire one way or the other. He was wearing what looked like a body warmer and thin black trousers; not exactly a follower of fashion thought Ruff.

"I'm sorry, we do not have any men's magazines for you to look at so would you please leave," the shopkeeper demanded.

"No, love, I'm here about Lady Pottersby," said Ruff.

All of a sudden, his demeanour changed. "What about her, has there been an accident?" he asked.

"No, she asked me to look into the murder of the young lass Evelyn Trubshaw, she worked for you, didn't she?" asked Ruff.

"Yes, she did, please come in the back. I'm sorry, I thought you were a customer."

Ruff headed toward the back, squeezing his huge frame through the small hole so he could get to the back area. The man led Ruff into the back, it was a small area, obviously his living quarters. There were stairs leading upwards and a small kitchen again probably designed for one person, there was also a living room designed for one very small person. "Please do be sitting down, my good man," asked the shopkeeper.

"Thanks, love," said Ruff.

"Can I be getting you a drink tea or coffee?"

"Coffee, love, seven sugars," said Ruff.

"Seven sugars, have you never heard of cholesterol?" said the shopkeeper. After some time passed, the little man appeared and placed the tray down on the table containing cakes and sweets and also the two coffees. "Make sure there is no mix up, I do not want seven sugars. I do not think I could drink anything with seven sugars, I'm not sure anyone should." Ruff leaned over and grabbed a pink cake in his sausage fingers and proceeded to drink his coffee. As the coffee left the cup and went into his mouth, the shopkeeper let out an exclamation, "Ooh, Jesus, are you sure you are not needing an ambulance after drinking that?" he announced.

"No, I'm fine. Tell me about Evelyn," said Ruff.

"Evelyn was a wonderful girl and she had a bright future ahead of her, she was planning on going to college to study catering, she was just helping out here to make some money. She had a small car and things cost so much these days and people like their independence," said the shopkeeper.

"Did she have a boyfriend?" asked Ruff.

"She had no time for boys, she said sex only messes up your mind, she was waiting till she got married," said the shopkeeper.

"Did she have an argument with anyone?" asked Ruff.

"There was a man at the college, I think it was one of her teachers, he made advances toward her, and she said she would report him," said the shopkeeper.

"Did she?" asked Ruff.

"No, because the teacher claimed no one would believe her. So, one day she got a tape and waited until after class and waited for her teacher to come on again; she recorded the whole thing," said the shopkeeper.

Ruff looked happy as though he was finally getting somewhere. "So where is the tape?" asked Ruff.

"I don't know but she had a friend, maybe she gave it to her," said the shopkeeper.

Ruff was hoping the answer would be what he wanted. "Who was her friend?" asked Ruff.

"It was the lady just murdered, Bertha Breasts," said the shopkeeper.

"How did they become friends?" asked Ruff.

"When she began work at the mansion, no one would talk to her because they were all so upper class. One day she was asked to prepare a meal in the kitchen. Well, as you know, Lady Pottersby only allows a very small circle of people into her house, so of course no one could help her as she knew nothing about cooking. From what she told me, she was so upset, she began crying and someone must have heard her. You ever heard the lyrics to a song, even in the darkest night, someone is at your side? Well, the door opened, and Miss Bertha walked in, even in bad people there is always one good and Bertha was that. She helped prepare a meal and kept silent, leaving Lady Pottersby thinking that Evelyn had done the whole thing. Evelyn felt she had a real friend, so when she feared for her safety, I would guess the most logical thing was to..." said the shopkeeper.

"Give the tape to her," Ruff finished.

"Yes," said the shopkeeper.

"Can I use your phone please, love?" asked Ruff.

"Of course, I do not believe in mobiles, so it is a landline on the table there," said the shopkeeper.

Ruff got up off the settee after three attempts and wobbled over to the phone, bending down to pick it up and giving the shopkeeper full view of his crack. "Cover it up, please!" shouted the shopkeeper as Ruff tried to cover it with his shirt.

Ruff dialled the number and got through to Jarvis. "Hello, love, think I've got a lead, something to do with a tape, tell Lady Pottersby."

With that, he put down the phone and turned round. "Anything you can tell me about this teacher, love?" said Ruff.

"He works at Moontown College, I think he teaches English, his name is Mr Puktar," said the shopkeeper.

"Will they see me?" asked Ruff.

"Probably leave it until morning but I would make an appointment, be careful what you say," said the shopkeeper.

"How do you mean, love?" asked Ruff.

"Think about it. If these two murders have been committed because of this tape, and he did kill them, and he does not yet have it back, and he also knows you are looking for it, then, my obese friend, you too could find yourself in danger," said the shopkeeper.

"Aye, OK, thanks, love," said Ruff.

Ruff returned to the mansion with his head full of new leads. So, was this teacher behind it all? But one thing did still puzzle him, if it was the teacher, knowing how Lady Pottersby was about strangers, how did he get into this mansion? And also, sticking three meat hooks into someone would require great strength, so either this man was incredibly strong or there was a second man or woman. Tomorrow would be fun thought Ruff.

Once again, the morning arrived all too soon and Ruff was awoken by Jarvis of all people. "Excuse me, sir," said Jarvis.

"Eh up, love, I'm in me pants," said Ruff trying desperately to cover up.

"Sorry to bother you, sir, but I just wanted to let you know that your appointment has been confirmed at the college with Mr Puktar for 10 o'clock."

"Thanks, love," said Ruff.

Ruff headed out again on his bike past the village and into the small area of countryside that enveloped the area of Moontown. Moontown was unique in that most places, when they had greenery, people would just cut them down and build more houses; however, with Moontown, the countryside still existed. As Ruff finally made his way past the trees, the other end of Moontown greeted him. It was more of an industrialised area with a lot of nuclear power plants and more big-name shops than in the other end, which was basically a few small shops. The college lay just on the edge of Moontown, and was a big, imposing grey building which from the outside looked like a hospital. As Ruff got toward the college, he sidled up to one of the bike racks, locking up his bike, as when you were built like him, the last thing you wanted to do was walk as it was like asking for a heart attack. Ruff approached the big double doors which automatically opened as he made his way into the foyer. The reception area of the college was very large, there were not many tables, but one huge desk occupied by a woman with steel-rimmed spectacles and a stern look on her face. To the left and right of Ruff were stairs leading up to the second floor, but much to his dismay, no lift. If there really was no lift thought Ruff, Mr Puktar was coming down the stairs as he simply could not get up.

"Can I help you, sir, cookery class is it?" she asked.

"No, love, I've come to see a teacher," said Ruff.

"Can I ask your name please," asked the lady.

"Ruff."

"Very good dog impersonation, sir, but I will need your full name or I cannot put you through," she said.

"Ruff rs."

"Well really," she said indignantly, "what is your real name and how are you spelling it."

"Ruff rs, spelt R S, pronounced arse, check on your computer," he said.

"I will check, sir, but I can assure you that there is—" She stopped mid-sentence and began to stammer, "I, er." She handed him a card. "Here is your ID card, sir, it tells people who you are. I simply refuse to put what you have told me there so I'm calling you Paul, that is IF you still wish to see Mr Puktar," she said.

"Don't want to see him, love, I need to see him. Lady Pottersby sent me."

At that point, her face turned ashen. "Lady Pottersby, oh well, that does change things, yes it does, can I help at all?"

"Aye, love, you got any lifts? I'm not making them stairs," he said.

"Of course, sir. Mr Puktar, get your arse down here, someone from Lady Pottersby. Please take a seat."

Ruff sat down on one of the chairs, his immense bulk almost destroying it, he leaned forward grabbing a magazine but all he found were gossip magazines and that is the last thing he wanted. He leant forward again, knocking something onto the floor, thank goodness he thought, a comic. He threw the books on the table and picked up the comic and began to read, his huge bulk shaking the chair every time he laughed. As he reached the end of his comic, Mr Puktar arrived. "Are you Mr Ruff?" he enquired as he extended his hand.

"Aye, love, I've come to talk to you about Evelyn."

"Evelyn?" said Puktar.

"Evelyn Trubshaw," said Ruff. The blood drained out of Puktar's face.

"Why should I know anything about her?" he stammered.

"It's OK, love, I've been told everything. I just need a few blanks filling in," said Ruff.

"Blanks?" said Puktar bemused.

"Blanks like she was your student, were you trying to bang her then?" said Ruff.

Mr Puktar looked at Ruff. "It's a bit coarse, don't you think?" said Puktar.

"Were you?" asked Ruff.

"She was an attractive girl and we both felt the same way," said Puktar.

"Aye, love, if I could stop you there, I know about the tape," said Ruff.

Once again, the blood left Puktar's face. "The tape."

"Aye, did you find it then?" said Ruff.

There was a silence and all emotion left Puktar's face. Finally, he let out a smirk. "Can I get you a drink?"

"Aye, coffee, love, seven sugars," said Ruff.

"Seven sug—?" said Puktar. "Do you mind me asking, do you have any teeth?"

"So, the tape; did you find it?" repeated Ruff.

"I think it was more of a threat, I don't think the tape actually ever existed," said Puktar.

"If it did, though, you would certainly want it back," said Ruff.

"If I did, would you be in a position to help?" said Puktar.

"Nah, love, I'm here to find out why she was murdered," said Ruff.

"Murdered! I had no idea. When?" said Puktar with an air of surprise in his voice.

"Aye, I'm sure you didn't know about Bertha either," said Ruff.

At that moment two coffees arrived. "Who is the diabetic?" said the canteen lady.

"Mines the seven sugars, love," said Ruff as he attempted to grab the cup. Placing the cups down the lady walked away. At that point, Puktar put the cup to his mouth and began to drink.

"Bertha Breasts," said Ruff. At that point, coffee flew out of Puktar's mouth as he began to choke. Finally, he regained his composure.

"Who?" he gasped.

"That was her name. She was murdered with three meat hooks, one through the head and two through her breasts."

Puktar looked at Ruff as he began to drink and then collapsed back in his chair. Suddenly two security guards appeared. "We need him out of here," said Puktar.

The two security guards attempted to lift him, but Ruff weighed nearly 25 stone and would not move easily. "You're going to need a forklift to get this bugger off the ground," said the security guard. As he said that, people started to gather.

"It's OK, everyone, just a fat man fallen asleep, let's let him sleep it off," said Puktar. Mr Puktar walked over to reception. "I need a break, I need you to arrange me two tickets to anywhere, so long as it's far away. Also, call the emergency services and tell them we have a large, collapsed fat man at the college needing urgent medical attention; if they ask his weight say 20 plus at a guess."

At the college two ambulances appeared and found Ruff sleeping, four ambulance men tried to lift him but failed, in the end they gave up. One of the ambulancemen got on the radio. "Emergency copter needed, one extraction, very fat man, may need wheels and harness, any local strongmen fancy a challenge?" The call went out and fortunately for the college, there was a local circus in town with a strongman named Marvo. After about 15 attempts, they managed to drag him outside and into a waiting harness, finally arriving at hospital.

After some time, Ruff awoke. "Where am I?"

"You are in hospital, I think you were drugged," said the doctor.

"Aye, reckon it was that teacher what did it," said Ruff.

"What teacher might that be?" asked the doctor.

"Mr Puktar from the local college," said Ruff.

"Nurse, get onto the police and tell them there is a teacher who likes to drug people," said the doctor.

"So how long will I be in then, Doc?" asked Ruff.

"Well, I can't really see anything wrong with you at all, apart from your immense weight. I guess you can go when you're ready," said the doctor.

Ruff finally returned back to the mansion and found Lady Pottersby and began to explain all that had happened to him that day and all about the mysterious Mr Puktar from the college. Lady Pottersby looked at Ruff. "So what happens now?" she asked.

"Well, assuming the tape's real, I guess Puktar could be our murderer. But how he got into your mansion and why he removed the hand is still a mystery," said Ruff.

"You have done very well, and I think you need some rest," said Lady Pottersby.

Ruff looked at her. "I don't think rest is something I need after being drugged, but I will go to bed as it's night-time," said Ruff.

"What about Puktar?" said Lady Pottersby.

"I need more, I need some evidence. The only person who can corroborate the tape is dead, so maybe someone who knew her. I know, Colonel Buttocks," said Ruff, "I'll talk to him in the morning."

Once again morning came, and Ruff felt very Ruff as the sunlight poured through the window. Sun was common in Moontown but not like this, this morning the sun was blazing. Ruff went downstairs to the kitchen and made himself a coffee and some bagels with bacon and egg. To an outsider, it looked revolting, to Ruff it was ambrosia of the Gods themselves. Colonel Buttocks made his way into the kitchen and made his way over to Ruff, he sat down next to him and began to speak, "I hope this is not more fun about my name, I am proud to be Barrington Buttocks."

After suppressing a laugh, Ruff explained about the second murder of Miss Breasts and his concern that she may have taken a lot of information to the grave. "What can I say? Yes, I knew of the blighter. Evelyn was a sweet girl. You see, I was brought up in a strict military family; don't do this, act this way not that, lights out 10 o'clock, yes, it was hard work growing up a Buttock. When my parents died, I tried to adopt a normal life and become a regular run-of-the-mill citizen, but have you any idea how hard it is? When your life is one of strict regime, of doing as you're told and only talking to the poshest of the posh, changing attitudes is like asking someone to become a new person. But Evelyn was a very likeable girl, I was ready to go and give that shifty blighter what for, but

Lady Pottersby dissuaded me, saying it would be a blemish on my character for an army colonel to be seen helping a simple girl like that. So, against my better judgement, I did not get involved," he said.

"What about the tape?" asked Ruff.

"Well, apparently, she made a tape of his advances, which I thought was dangerous if the damn blighter found out, but she decided to go ahead and do it anyway. As far as I am aware, she brought it back and I think she gave it to Bertha for safekeeping, and then Bertha goes and gets herself murdered, one can only assume for the tape," said the colonel.

"If I could somehow connect the two with a motive, I'd have Puktar, but all I have is he tried to have an affair and she made a tape of his advances, but who has the tape?" said Ruff.

"Puktar," said the colonel.

"It's possible, even probable, he did drug me; there must have been a reason," said Ruff.

"If you want the advice of an old man, we take my car and we squeeze the information out of the blighter anyway we can," said the colonel.

"It's a plan," said Ruff, "OK, let's go."

So, Ruff and the colonel got into his car. The colonel's car was a classic car, probably from the 30s thought Ruff, even earlier maybe. It was a car that required a starting handle, a bit of a pain but it was his car and he was proud of it.

"Come on, man, squeeze them buttocks in," he said as Ruff desperately tried to get his lower half in the door. Finally, most of him was in and the colonel drove off with Ruff holding the door closed, praying they hit nothing that would send him flying onto the road. But as the car gathered speed, it only went about 20, so there was no danger to Ruff. After a long time, the two men arrived at the college, ready to meet with Mr Puktar. Again, the same problem greeted Ruff as he desperately tried to squeeze his bottom half out the door. "Have you ever thought of a diet, you fat blighter?" announced the colonel.

"I am a rough-arse building worker I am meant to be fat," said Ruff.

The two men entered the college and made their way to the reception desk. "We are here to see Mr Puktar," said the colonel.

"Do you have an appointment?" she asked.

"I don't need an appointment, you cheeky young pup, I shall have you across my knee in a minute. Announce us, will you, I am Barrington Buttocks and you know my friend. The receptionist began to giggle. "Would you like me to report you?" said the colonel. "I am a highly decorated and respected colonel and this, and this, well the less said about him the better, but I still want to see him. Which room does he reside in?" said the colonel.

"He is in room 24, but he is teaching," said the receptionist.

"Well, he is about to be taught something by Colonel Barrington Buttocks." The colonel stormed up the stairs two at a time with a face like thunder. You could hear his grunting noises crashing through the silent air, then complete silence.

A few minutes passed and then the colonel reappeared. "What's the matter, love?" asked Ruff to the colonel.

The colonel sat down, looking dishevelled. The receptionist ran over with a glass of water. "Here, drink this."

The colonel took a big gulp and then spoke. "He's dead, the blighter's hanged himself," said the colonel.

Slowly, Ruff went up the stairs, only one at a time, pausing for breath at every opportunity. When he finally made it, he found Mr Puktar hanging from his neck attached to a fan. Near the body of Puktar was a knife. Ruff opened it and managed to cut him down and got the shock of his life, for when he removed the rope, there were no ligature marks; he had been placed there by someone, the question was who? Ruff came down the stairs very slowly.

"Did you see the blighter?" said the colonel.

"Yes, but it wasn't what I thought," said Ruff.

"How do you mean?" asked the colonel.

Ruff stayed silent until he got outside. As they were driving back to the mansion, Ruff finally broke his silence. "He did not commit suicide, someone put him there," said Ruff.

"You mean we were made to think it was suicide, so how did he die?" said the colonel.

"I can only assume he was strangled, but we will have to wait for the results of the post-mortem," said Ruff as the car headed back toward the mansion.

Ruff poured out two cups of coffee and sat down with the colonel. "So, what do we have so far?" asked the colonel.

"Two dead bodies, they seem that they may be connected to a third dead body that we assumed was suicide but in fact was murder," said Ruff.

"Which means what?" said the colonel.

"It means that whoever is doing this is trying to throw us off the scent, not just once but again and again," said Ruff.

"Tell me something, what did you learn on your murder mystery weekend?" asked the colonel.

"I guess the most important thing we learned was, never assume, find out for yourself," said Ruff.

"Well, let's assume that Mr Puktar killed them both, for that tape. Where does that leave us now?" asked the colonel.

Ruff pondered for a moment without speaking. "I started to think it was for the tape, but if that's the case the person whose life was threatened most by the tape is dead," said Ruff.

"Which leaves?" said the colonel, Ruff looked at him.

"Another killer," said Ruff.

"Precisely, you have been going after the wrong person and the right person," said the colonel.

"I don't understand," said Ruff. The colonel reached into his top pocket and produced a pen and then went to one of the drawers and pulled out a notepad which they used to write menus on.

"You assumed after what had happened, you had everything in place, all you needed was a connection between the tape and Mr Puktar. Now, you assumed the connection was he would lose his job for harassing a pupil, but maybe there was someone else who stood to lose a lot more if the link was made, so they severed the link by making it look like a suicide. You buy the suicide and then the killer has killed himself, case closed, and the real killer gets away," said the colonel.

"So what you're trying to say, love, is I got too close," said Ruff.

"You got way too close, and tomorrow you start again from the start with a fresh approach," said the colonel.

"Why?" asked Ruff.

"Because you nearly made it and you got so close you scared the real killer, so what we need is to go in a different path so the killer thinks—" said the colonel.

"I have a new direction and a new clue taking me further away from him or her," said Ruff.

"Exactly, and hopefully this will draw them out before someone else gets killed," said the colonel. The colonel drew himself up and began to leave.

"Can I ask you one last thing before you go to bed?" said Ruff.

"Ask," said the colonel.

"Where does Bertha fit into this and the hand?" said Ruff.

The colonel turned and sat back down. "The hand, I'm not certain, but I think it was meant to be a distraction, but as for poor old Bertha, I think it was the friendship between her and Evelyn that caused her death; the killer was looking for something and either found it or Bertha refused to surrender it and it cost her life," said the colonel.

Once again, another night passed, and Ruff found himself in the kitchen with the colonel. "What happens today, love?" said Ruff.

"I have given it much thought in bed, and I think today we catch the killer," said the colonel.

"How?" said Ruff expectantly.

"I don't know but it's something I've always wanted to say," said the colonel. Ruff's expression changed to one of gloom. "Don't get depressed, we will find the killer in the end, hopefully before someone else dies, now how are we doing with the interviews?" asked the colonel.

"Not so good, we have interviewed about four out of 100. Any suggestion who is next?" asked Ruff.

"Let's have a look at your list," asked the colonel. Ruff handed the list over and the colonel scanned all the names until he came to one that stuck in his mind. "Try this one," he said, pointing at the list.

Ruff looked at the name, Simon Mere. "Who is he?" asked Ruff.

"His father worked for the college; he knew everyone there. When his father died, he had just finished training to be a teacher and had been at the college. He worked as a teacher and a trainee in administration."

Simon Mere appeared wearing a yellow suit with grey trousers, he looked in his mid-twenties with slick, combed-back hair. He would be about five foot eight and had a wry smile on his face as though he knew something, but whatever it was, he was keeping it to himself.

"Mr Mere, please sit down," said Ruff.

Simon sat down across the table from Ruff, looking uncomfortable. "I suppose it's about the murders," said Simon.

"Can you tell us anything that might help, love?" asked Ruff.

"On the night of the murder I was in the mansion, but I heard something I was not supposed to," said Simon.

"Why do you say that, Simon?" asked the colonel.

"Because it was told in whispered tones, it was to do with a cassette," he said.

Ruff started to look interested as did the colonel. "What about the tape?" asked Ruff.

"I did not see into the room so I cannot be sure about this, but it sounded like a man and a woman arguing. It was about 10.30 at night, I know this as it woke me up. The woman was saying *I have hidden the tape in the mansion but you will never find it*, the man was saying, *I already know, Bertha has it*, then it became violent, and it sounded as though the man had hit the woman. I could not get involved or it would have blown my cover," said Simon.

"Go on," said Ruff.

"Well, I went back to bed, and about half eleven, it started again, but this time I heard the man say, *you tell me, or you won't see the morning*," said Simon.

"Tell me what?" said the colonel.

"Exactly, I don't know, just that, that was the last time I heard anything," said Simon.

"Well, thank you for your help and maybe some more questions later," said Ruff.

"I am around if you need me," said Simon.

He exited the room as the colonel looked at Ruff. "Well, what do you think?" he asked.

"Well, all it tells us is that there is a man making threats and he possibly killed Evelyn, and I do say possibly. I think we need to visit the mortuary and find out how Mr Puktar died," said Ruff.

The two men rose to their feet and headed back outside when all of a sudden, a scream tore through the air. "It's coming from Lucy's bedroom." The two men rushed back inside to Lucy's bedroom or to be more precise the colonel rushed in and Ruff waddled in like a duck. "Hang on, love," said Ruff to the colonel. When they arrived, the scene was one of carnage. Lady Pottersby was stood over the body of Lucy, she was half-naked and covered in blood, her breasts had been sliced clean off.

Immediately, Ruff grabbed Lady Pottersby. "How many more must die, Ruff?" she asked.

"Hopefully, no more, Lady Pottersby. I started this and I'm going to get to the end, the colonel and I will catch the killer."

Part Four

One Thousand Roses

Ruff squeezed himself into the colonel's car and squeezed out at the mortuary. As they went inside, the familiar smell of formaldehyde filled the air. "Good morning, my lovelies," said the mortician as they entered.

"Someone is cheery, sir," said the colonel.

"It's a horrible job to do if you're not cheery, sir, I challenge you to try it," said the mortician. The mortician was called Ralph and probably should have retired a few years ago, he was in his late seventies, but age to him was just a number. He asked himself, could you do the job? If the answer was yes, then hell, why should you retire? Ralph could have challenged Ruff in a weight contest, he would probably have lost but then again not by much; his fat was mostly around the waist as he admitted he ate too much. His sense of humour was definitely not suitable for the job he had. His face had a rugged, lived-in look but remarkably very few wrinkles considering his age, he always claimed that God had given him a biological steam iron that he used every day to devastating effect. His biggest feature was his teeth, late seventies and all his own, he also believed in dyeing his hair so that when his time did finally come, he could meet his maker looking as snappy as possible. He had a long, pointy nose and glasses which always perched on the end like a college professor, seeing him most people wanted to warn him they were about to fall off, fortunately they never did.

"So, we have come to see Mr Puktar," said the colonel.

"Ah, which one of you is Ruff?" he said, Ruff raised his hand.

"Well, my friend, I think you are right," said Ralph.

"Am I?" said a surprised Ruff.

"Yes, it definitely was not a suicide, you can see under the light there are no ligature marks; if he had hanged himself, there would have been rope burns, someone wanted to lead you down the wrong path and make you think it was a suicide," said the mortician.

"Why?" asked the colonel.

"I'm afraid I cannot answer that question, all I can do is tell you how he did die and hope it helps," said the mortician.

"Which is?" asked Ruff.

"Poisoning, some kind of weed killer it looks like, I would have to run more tests on it, but I would be surprised if I am wrong," said Ralph.

"So, someone hanged him and then drugged him," said the colonel.

"No," said Ralph. "He was never hanged, there was a struggle and his neck was damaged, not enough to kill him but enough to render him unconscious with pain, then the drug, then the rope to make it look like suicide," said Ralph.

"What about the others?" said Ruff.

"All poisoned," said Ralph, "come back here with me if your stomach be strong, me hearties," said Ralph.

"Sorry?" said Ruff.

"I always fancied being a pirate," said Ralph.

"We begin with Evelyn," Ralph pulled back the sheet showing the body of Evelyn in full view with her missing hand. "As you pointed out, Ruff, she had a powder on her lips, this powder was the weed killer. Even though her neck was slashed, again it was to draw the attention away from the real cause," said Ralph.

"You mean?" said Ruff.

"Yes, the neck was slashed after the drug had already killed her," said Ralph.

"What about Bertha?" asked Ruff.

"This is a good one," said Ralph as he threw back the sheets causing Ruff to go pale. "She had a hook in each breast and a hook through the top of her head, but as you know a post-mortem examines the lot, so I cut open all her organs and found traces of the drug in her stomach," said Ralph.

"The same drug," said Ruff.

"The same, the breasts and head were mutilated after the event and not before, she was dead before it happened," said Ralph.

"Lucy," said Ruff.

Ralph whipped back the third sheet showing Lucy's naked body but with no breasts. "Again, same thing, this drug, whatever it is, caused death then she was mutilated," said Ralph.

Ralph replaced the sheets as the three men left the room. As Ralph closed the door to the fridge, Ruff asked the obvious question.

"Why?" said Ruff.

"You mean, why kill these people by poisoning and then mutilate them?" said Ralph. "I have two theories, one is that whatever the drug is will lead you to identify the killer immediately, so he mutilates the body to send you the wrong way," said Ralph.

"The second," said Ruff.

"The second is a horrible thought," said Ralph.

"Which is?" said the colonel.

"There may be no reason at all, it could simply be he or she is enjoying killing and simply won't stop. He will kill anyone or anything, which means trying to catch them would literally involve you catching them in the act," said Ralph.

The two men walked together out of the mortuary together. "So, what now?" asked Ruff.

"We need to find that poison, and maybe it is the key? You heard what he said, whoever is doing this does not want us to find out who it is, and the poison could help us find the killer," said the colonel.

"I am starting to think that maybe it is not one of Lady Pottersby's friends," said Ruff.

"Don't forget the tape, it is the only lead we have, if we could find that then maybe the contents will reveal the killer to us," said the colonel.

"Maybe not, you heard them say that she recorded the tape of some bloke chasing her around the room or trying it on; would a recording of that really help?" asked Ruff.

The two men drove back to the mansion, as they arrived, they were greeted by many cars on the gravel driveway. "Lady Pottersby, who are these blighters?" asked the colonel.

"I have decided to have a banquet, so I invited a few of my friends, hopefully it will cheer the place up after all the doom and gloom," said Lady Pottersby.

"M'lady, do you think it's wise considering there is a possibility that the killer is in the house somewhere?" said the colonel.

"Nonsense. You, Jarvis and Ruff will protect us from this swine," said Lady Pottersby.

As she turned toward the house to walk off, Ruff looked at the colonel and whispered, "Who looks after us?" The colonel hung his head and shook it in a defeated pose.

As Ruff and the colonel entered the house, immediately they were hit by a heavy throng of voices chattering away. Some were distinct and some were distinctly distorted, but the odd word flashed across the entranceway, *murder, oh yes, not been caught yet, some builder.*

"Why do I get the feeling I am walking into a trap?" said Ruff.

"You probably are, old boy. Remember, there is a good chance that girl was killed because she knew something she shouldn't or had something she shouldn't; what if it's the same with you?" said the colonel.

"Let's say this, if it's one of us next, the remaining one must protect her ladyship. Agreed?" said Ruff.

"Agreed, old boy. You know, you're not such a cad after all," said the colonel. As time wound down and day gave way to the night, the party started. IT was a banquet to end all banquets, there was food of every description, roast pig, roast chicken, roast pheasant, there was much champagne flowing and many side dishes for those who simply could not stomach a large meal. As the meal carried on, so did the conversation, but like a needle stuck on a record, it was always the same topic: the murder and whodunnit, would it ever be solved and who was Ruff? In fact, Ruff and the colonel were not enjoying the meal but watching on from afar hoping nothing would happen, but realising that if it did, it would probably be soon and more than likely involve the banquet. As the banquet reached its maximum, Jarvis took a break and went to find his friends. "What do you think, sir?" said Jarvis.

"I am pretty sure it will happen here; I just wish I could be more prepared, love," said Ruff.

"Don't worry; we will be ready for the blighters, eh what," said the colonel as once again a scream tore through the floors of the mansion.

Racing upstairs once again to another bedroom, the colonel walked into the bedroom to find the body of one of the guests, decapitated and lying on a bed of what looked like a thousand roses. As Ruff's body finally waddled up the stairs, even he was shocked by what was now becoming a regular occurrence.

"Okay, why?" said the colonel.

"Why, what?" asked Ruff.

"Why, the decapitation and, more importantly, why the roses?" said the colonel.

Ruff bent down to look at the body, and a big shudder went up as everyone in the room averted their eyes from the sight of his builder's cleavage. "Well, I got a few things from the body," said Ruff.

"So did we, Ruff, from you. Why can't you wear trousers that fit?" said Lady Pottersby.

"Sorry, love," said Ruff hitching up his jeans.

"Go on," said the colonel.

"Judging by her hands, I would say she is young as she has no wrinkles, either that or she uses one hell of a wrinkle cream. Also, it wasn't sexual," said Ruff.

"How do you know?" asked Lady Pottersby.

Ruff moved some of the roses adorning her body, revealing what was underneath. "She still has her panties on," said Ruff.

"Why did the blighter decapitate her and why the roses?" said the colonel.

"The roses, I am not sure, but I guess the decapitation was to stop us identifying her, but I am sure our friend at the mortuary will help us with that," said Ruff.

A few more days passed, and Ruff and the colonel found themselves back at the mortuary once again. "Ladies and gentlemen, presenting my two most frequent visitors Ruff, Buttocks," said Ralph.

"That's Colonel Buttocks if you don't mind and less of the humour, young whippersnapper," said the colonel.

"Have you discovered anything?" asked Ruff.

"Many things; the first is that it was not a professional job," said Ralph.

"How so?" asked the colonel.

Ralph pulled back the sheets revealing the headless corpse. "If you look closely, gentlemen, you can see rough edges to the decapitation site. Whoever did this used some kind of saw or bread knife, if he had been professional, he would have used a blade and made a clean cut," said Ralph.

"Why?" asked the colonel.

"Again, evidence. Look closely, you can see ragged skin, there is your DNA. When the killer did this, bits of metal came off the saw blade, we have retrieved most of them, maybe we can find out what kind of a saw it is and then you can trace who sold it and maybe you will have a solid lead," said Ralph.

"The roses?" asked Ruff.

"Smell her?" asked Ralph.

"I beg your pardon, sir," said the colonel faced flushed with embarrassment.

"Smell her," repeated Ralph.

The colonel bent down and placed his nose near the body and began to retch. "My God, the blighter smells foul," said the colonel holding his nose.

"Exactly, she was murdered some time ago, the roses were to cover up the scent," said Ralph.

"If we could trace who sold the roses, it would help," said Ruff.

"It shouldn't be too hard, they are Dutch, we have had it confirmed from the laboratory. They are Rosa rugosa, species rose, they are also infected with thrips, she had them wandering about her body. Maybe it attracted maggots, which caused the decomposition," said Ralph.

"What are thrips?" asked Ruff.

"Thrips are a type of invisible plague to roses; you can see the damage to the petal edges," said Ralph.

"So how did they get on her?" asked the colonel.

Ralph walked over to the table and produced a glass jar containing winged insects and handed it to the colonel. "By gad, what are these blighters?" asked the colonel.

"Thrips, they are tiny winged insects that settle between the petals of tight buds and as you can see destroy the petal edges."

"The blighter never knew they had them?" asked the colonel.

"They are more visible on lighter-coloured roses, so it is conceivable he or she did not even know they had them," said Ralph.

The colonel handed the jar to Ruff. "Are they dangerous to humans?" said Ruff.

"In the sense that they cause a rash, if you're present when one is hatching, the hungry thrips will target humans, causing a rash or swelling. Look at her legs, it's possible that is why the killer removed the head, as it is likely that she had rashes and bites on her face. Or it could simply be to avoid detection, as if someone saw the face, they may know who it is, and they could tie it in with the killer," said Ralph.

"Thrips, eh?" said the colonel.

"I think there is a shop in the village that sells Dutch roses, we could ask there," said Ruff.

"Just a moment, if there were about one thousand roses there, her face must have been in some state with all those thrips biting her," said the colonel.

"I would guess so," said Ralph. "So, gentlemen, until the next body you bring me," said Ralph.

"Hopefully, there will be no more," said Ruff heading for the door.

The two men got outside. "You know I think he is enjoying this," said Ruff. Inside the car, the two men contemplated where they would go next.

"It has to be the florist, I assume," said the colonel as his car sped down the street.

Arriving at the florist, Ruff exited the car with as much dignity as he could muster, then he and the colonel entered the shop. Inside the florist shop was all manner of plants, large cacti, small cacti and flowers of every kind, yellow ones, red ones; it felt like being in a field, the smell of fresh flowers filled the air. Ruff and the colonel waited and then someone appeared. The shop assistant was a small man in his late fifties, his hairline was receding as were his teeth, as every time he smiled, you could see where they probably should have been. "Good day, gentlemen, how may I help you, do you wish to purchase?"

"No, we're detectives, and we want to talk to you about thrips," said Ruff.

The shop assistant wore glasses which may have been too strong for him as he was constantly looking over the top of them. "I know no one called thrips, sir, why what has he done?" asked the shopkeeper.

"Thrips are invisible nasties that live in roses. We have reason to believe you may have sold some roses contaminated with thrips, not intentionally we understand," said Ruff.

The shopkeeper looked as though he was about to explode as his face became more flushed. "Such words, sir! I would never sell such a product, intentionally or otherwise, now I wish you to leave my premises," said the shopkeeper.

"No, you scoundrel, you will answer our questions, damn your eyes," said the colonel as he raised his walking cane.

The shopkeeper squealed in fear and hid behind Ruff as he was nearly as big as the desk. "OK, love, we're not here for violence, we just want answers," said Ruff picking up the small man and placing him on the desk like a doll.

"We work for Lady Pottersby, and there have been some murders up at the mansion. She and ourselves would like them to stop, but I guess the killer has other ideas, so if you could help us find who bought this stuff or indeed who you sold it to, I would appreciate it," said Ruff.

"Lady Pottersby, is she in danger?" asked the shopkeeper.

"We don't know, it's possible. We don't know the killer, every time we get a lead, our lead seems to die, and we are back at square one," said Ruff.

"Where are you now, would you say?" asked the shopkeeper.

"Probably square two as we have leads but they are going nowhere," said Ruff.

"I sold those flowers to Mr Puktar," said the shopkeeper.

"What is your name? Just for our records," asked Ruff.

"Amir Klamp," said the shopkeeper.

"That is an unusual name," said Ruff.

"What is your name if you don't mind me asking?" said Amir.

"I am Ruff."

"Do you have a second name?" asked Amir.

"Arse."

"So, it would appear, Mr Arse, your name is more stupid than mine," said Amir.

"I never said your name was stupid, I just said unusual," said Ruff.

"You sir?" asked Amir looking at the colonel. *Here we go,* thought Ruff.

"Buttocks, sir, Colonel Barrington Buttocks."

"Gentlemen, we have a winner," said Amir.

"How do you mean?" asked Ruff.

"You say my name's stupid," said Amir.

"I didn't, I just said—" said Ruff.

"Let's get back to the job in hand, shall we?" asked the colonel.

"The person you sold the roses to just happens to be dead," said Ruff.

"You asked who I sold them to, there is your answer, I am sorry if you do not like it, but there is your answer," said Amir.

The two men left the shop and walked back to the car. "So, what happens now?" asked Ruff.

"In what respect, sir?" said the colonel.

"The man who was going to be our killer just happens to be dead, killed by someone else, what does that tell us?" asked Ruff.

"It tells us that he sold the plants on to someone else," said the colonel.

"That person is the killer," said Ruff.

"Not necessarily," said the colonel, "you see it is just possible that the person who bought those roses, bought them in good faith, it does happen you know, people do like to buy roses."

The two men arrived back at the mansion and immediately went to see Lady Pottersby to tell her about the latest developments. "Thrips, yes, I have heard of them, but I usually use a spray or suchlike to get rid of them."

Suddenly, Ruff thought of something. "Ere, love, where do you keep your weed killer?"

"Out in the potting shed, why?" said Lady Pottersby.

Ruff waddled down the stairs to find the colonel slumped in his armchair. "Colonel, I've found something," said Ruff.

The colonel shot to his feet. "Damn vermin, I'll shoot the lot of them." Ruff grabbed hold of the colonel.

"Relax, sir, it's me Ruff."

"Oh, it's you, what do you want?" he asked.

"I may possibly have a lead. Lady Pottersby uses a weed killer to kill thrips, what if the weed killer is missing?" said Ruff.

"Come on," said the colonel as he rushed to the potting shed.

The potting shed was in a state of somewhat disrepair with some of the panes of glass needing replacing and some of the plants ready to die. In a safe marked Private stood a combination lock, Ruff guessed the weed killer was in there. Ruff came out of the potting shed and back into the house to find Jarvis the butler going about his daily chores. "Jarvis, what is the combination to the potting shed safe?" said Ruff. He went back outside and used the combination to open the barrel lock and open the safe. Inside the rusty green safe was a bottle marked Weed Killer. Is this what the killer used?

Part Five

A Mix Up

Ruff put on gloves and took the bottle to the laboratory to get it identified but was told it would take a few days. Ruff headed back to the mansion and the kitchen to once again speak with the colonel to see if he had any new leads to give him. "Well, that's all done, the weed killer will be identified and then at least we will have something to work with," said Ruff.

"How do you mean, sir?" asked the colonel.

"The weed killer, they use it to kill thrips, someone has used the weed killer not just to kill thrips but to kill humans as well," said Ruff.

"It's a splendid idea but just one problem," said the colonel.

"What?" said Ruff.

"Thrips are an insect and would be treated with insecticide spray not weed killer, weed killer is for weeds. I would imagine using weed killer on thrips would kill the roses," said the colonel.

"Shit," muttered Ruff.

"Shit or manure is very good for roses," said the colonel.

"No, I mean shit as in I've got it wrong, I assumed it would be weed killer," said Ruff.

"Never mind, we have more important things to do, we need to find more leads. I have spoken to a friend of mine and he says one of Lady Pottersby's guests was high," said the colonel.

"High as in drug high?" said Ruff.

"Precisely, sir," said the colonel.

"What does that have to do with the killer here?" asked Ruff.

"Nothing, I just can't stand drug dealers," said the colonel.

"I appreciate that, but I've got a killer to catch," said Ruff.

"Come with me, why don't you, it may help clear your head," said the colonel.

The two men got into the colonel's car again and drove off into the countryside until they arrived at a rather spacious looking farm, as Ruff extricated himself from the car, the colonel headed toward the main barn where the straw was kept. Ruff looked across the miles and miles of fields, each one held something different, some had wheat, some had corn. As Ruff followed the colonel to the main building, he could hear the cows mooing as though they were getting ready for their first milking of the day, also in the air he could hear the faint noise of horses neighing. The farm was big and open plan with very few buildings, just sheds containing either animals or farm machinery. As Ruff walked forwards, a young lady appeared. "May I help you, sir?" asked the lady in a very refined accent.

"Aye, love, we've come about the drugs," said Ruff in a not so refined accent.

"Sorry we neither purchase nor distribute drugs to people, good day," said the lady waving her hand motioning Ruff away.

"I don't think you understand, love," said Ruff.

"No, you don't understand, I have a large selection of pit bulls, would you like me to introduce them to you?"

Ruff did not know if she was serious, but he did not wish to find out. "Buttocks!" he shouted.

"I beg your pardon; how dare you use such language in the presence of a lady."

Once again, Ruff cried out, "Colonel Buttocks."

The response was swift but brutal as a cry for the dogs rang out. Just at that moment, Colonel Buttocks appeared around the corner. "Helen," said the colonel, the lady quickly turned her head to a voice she thought she knew.

"Oh, Barrington," she squealed. The two rushed to meet each other. Helen was a slender woman with chestnut coloured hair, she had a slim figure and was wearing a riding outfit and jodhpurs and holding a riding crop, but there was no sign of a horse, so whether this was to scare off people or whether this was her everyday attire was yet to be seen. "What are you doing here?" she asked.

"Brought the lad along as we are in the middle of an investigation, don't you know," said the colonel.

"He is so rude, calling out rude words," she said clinging onto him affectionately.

"Did he, by God, what did he say?"

"I don't want to repeat it, it was rude," she whispered eyeing Ruff with a look of disdain.

"Come on, my dear, you know me I am not easily shocked," said the colonel.

"He said buttocks," she squealed.

"Did he, by God!" As the colonel raised his stick halfway and then stopped.

"What's wrong?" she asked.

"He wasn't being rude, m'dear, that is my name," said the colonel.

Helen looked at Ruff then at the colonel. "Buttocks is that your name?" she asked.

"Yes, m'dear, Barrington Buttocks." Squeals and giggles rang out across the farm as the colonel stood looking totally nonplussed. "When you have quite finished, we have some questions for you," said the colonel.

"Yes of course," she paused and then spoke quickly before laughing again, "Buttocks."

"Colonel Buttocks if you please, my dear."

"So, what do you want to know?"

Ruff felt in order to speed this along and to avoid more hysterics, he would have to take over. "We understand you said that you saw one of Lady Pottersby's guests as high," said Ruff.

"Oh, yes, definitely. He had a blank expression, and his eyes were all emotionless and glazed over," said Helen.

"Where did the drugs come from, do you know?" said Ruff.

"No, but two things I do know; the drugs were on the premises already and two, I think, in fact, I am almost certain it was cannabis."

In Moontown, cannabis is highly illegal, and possession was punishable by death, so if someone was dealing in cannabis or indeed taking it, this was very serious. "What makes you think it was cannabis, love?" said Ruff.

"He was acting paranoid every time someone spoke to him, you could tell from his voice and his overall demeanour, this was cannabis."

"What makes you think that the drugs were on the premises, love," said Ruff.

"I was with him all evening; he was never high and then the next minute he appeared, and he was zoned out."

Ruff took down the information and got ready to leave. "Thank you, love," said Ruff as he headed to the car.

"Just a moment," she squealed, "what is your name?"

"Ruff rs," he said, at which point Helen entered hysterics from which she probably will never recover.

Ruff and the colonel headed back to the mansion in his car as the two men discussed the new information they now had. "So, assuming she was correct about the drugs being in the mansion, what do we do now?" asked Ruff.

"First job, we need to find evidence of drugs, then we need to stop the source," said the colonel.

"Do you think this could be a motive?" asked Ruff.

"It is possible. You know as well as I, peddling drugs in Moontown, especially cannabis, is punishable by death. So, would it not stand to reason that if indeed someone was peddling drugs, they would have to destroy any evidence which connected them or they could find themselves on the end of a rope," said the colonel.

The plot was starting to make more sense thought Ruff, we even had a motive now but still who was the killer, and more importantly, what they had was circumstantial; what they needed was something concrete that they could use in a court of law.

Arriving back at the mansion, the two men sat down in the kitchen only to be joined by Lady Pottersby who sat down with them. "Do you have any news at all which could crack this case open?" asked Lady Pottersby now speaking like a detective.

"Drugs," came back Ruff.

"Drugs?" she replied.

"Drugs," said the colonel.

"How, why, what makes you think?" she asked.

Ruff explained about Helen and her fits of hysteria at the mere mention of the colonel's name and how she had observed someone at the party who did at least appear to be on drugs but could it be proved? As for Lady Pottersby, she knew nothing about drugs, the mere mention of them upset her. "You do realise what you are saying? If you are caught with drugs in Moontown, you may as well kill yourself because if the police catch you, you're gone," she said.

"The fact is, love, I'm an amateur detective, I'm a builder by trade. I'm just trying to make some sense of all of this," said Ruff.

"What do you have that you can use?" said Lady Pottersby.

"Well, we have the drugs sighting, which is a motive in itself. If someone was peddling, surely they would attempt to cover it up? If they were found out, as you say, they are heading for a fry up, with themselves as the main dish," said Ruff.

"I don't know a lot about drugs, but would you not need to cultivate them somewhere? No one in Moontown has such facilities or the police would have discovered it," said Lady Pottersby.

"I'm like you, love, I know fu—, I mean I know nothing about drugs but I was always under the impression that drug plants were big things, and she said paranoid, which suggests cannabis," said Ruff.

"Cannabis plants in my house, oh no, no, I'm sorry, I can't believe that," said Lady Pottersby. "Anyway, would you not need some kind of hothouse, all I have is my old potting shed, aside from that is the boiler, which I guess would be far too hot for delicate plants. No, it's too silly for words," she concluded.

"Nevertheless, ma'am, we have to consider it as a possibility," said the colonel.

"Fine, consider it but please, do not take it seriously," said Lady Pottersby.

Once again, the daytime gave way to the night, and Pottersby mansion was plunged into darkness aside from the security lights outside. As Ruff lay in his bed, he could hear a wolf gently howling in the distance, and as it stopped, its voice gave way to an owl. First the wolf, then the owl, almost as though they were having a conversation with each other. Ruff knew he was no detective but he had been hired to do this job, and now he either had to go behind her ladyship's back and bring in the police against her wishes or try to solve it himself. *So*, thought Ruff, *what do I really have? Four dead bodies, all poisoned, a plant infected by thrips and hopefully tomorrow a positive answer from the laboratory about the possible contaminated weed killer.*

There is an old saying, another day another dollar, but for Ruff it was starting to sound like another day another murder. As the sun rose for the new day, the sunlight came streaming in through the curtains forcing Ruff onto his feet. Once again, he put his clothes on and headed down to the kitchen to see about any possible new developments in his world of murder. As he entered the kitchen, the colonel was already there holding a piece of paper. "Ah, Ruff, we have your sample back from the laboratory."

"Let me guess, it's weed killer."

"Yes and no, it's weed killer laced with something else – ammonia," said the colonel.

"Ammonia, but why?" asked Ruff.

"What does ammonia do?" asked the colonel.

"Apart from the smell, I don't really know, I am a building worker not a chemist," said Ruff.

"It's the smell; whoever did this was aiming at knocking out Lady Pottersby," said the colonel.

"Why Lady Pottersby?" said Ruff.

"I guess, for whatever reason, she is the next target or at least one of the next ones. Whoever the killer is, he or she must have realised that Lady Pottersby would scream as she does have a loud voice, so to avoid a struggle—"

"Knock her out," filled in Ruff.

"Well done, we'll make a detective of you yet, my boy," said the colonel.

"So, who is our target for today?" asked Ruff.

"The flower man; we need to find out what he knows about these bugs and how they affect cannabis plants."

The two men once again headed out looking for clues, hoping that today would bring about success. Finally, they arrived at the flower shop and everything appeared normal. Outside lots of hanging baskets in every colour you could imagine adorned the window as the sunlight bathed them showing off their beauty. Ruff and the colonel headed in as the door gave its familiar tinkle announcing their arrival. "Ah, Ruff, Buttocks, what can I be doing of assistance for you today?" asked Amir.

"Cannabis plants," said the colonel.

"Wrong person, gentlemen, I know the rules, those things are punishable by death under Moontown law, next question," said Amir.

"We are not accusing you, love, we want to know about them," said Ruff.

"I will try but I am not up to date on these things," said Amir.

Ruff pulled out a piece of paper with a name on. "Frankliniella accidentalis, what do you know about them?" said Ruff.

"They are yellowish-white flying bugs, and that's about it," said Amir.

"The effect on cannabis plants?" said the colonel.

Amir went to the back and pulled out a book, then he began to flick through some pages. "Here is something on your friend, these are the insects," he said, pointing out the bugs in the book.

"What is the effect on cannabis plants?" asked the colonel for the second time.

Amir took back his book and read the chapter thoroughly. "According to this, this particular strain of bug would destroy a cannabis plant, so if you're thinking of cultivating, gentlemen, I would keep these fellas away," said Amir.

"Thank you," said the colonel as the two men exited the shop.

"So, now what do we know?" asked the colonel.

"The same as before," said Ruff.

"No, we have a possible motive," said the colonel.

"We do?" said Ruff with a hint of surprise in his voice.

"Listen, my boy, no one would be crazy enough to cultivate this sort of plant in Moontown; you would get destroyed, your only hope would be to take it to someone who could cultivate without problems, someone associated with the royals," said the colonel.

"You don't mean Lady Pottersby?" said Ruff.

"I bet you somewhere in the mansion there is a cannabis cultivation centre which I intend to smash," said the colonel.

"So how do we find it?" asked Ruff.

"Tonight, when everyone is in bed, we go exploring," said the colonel.

Ruff shook his head, "I don't know about that, the last time I tried I nearly ended up being trapped underground in some weird tunnel."

"Possibly a dream," said the colonel.

"Possibly, but I could touch everything and feel everything," said Ruff.

"All I am saying is that I could not find a single thing in the mansion matching your description in any of the passages," said the colonel.

"So, I'm crazy," said Ruff.

The colonel looked at him. "Yes, I think you are completely round the bend, old boy, but this thing goes deeper than your personal paranoia," said the colonel. Like every day before it, the sun gave way to the moon and night was once again here, and while everyone was sleeping, Ruff and the colonel were on walkabout.

The two men pounded the mansion looking for something, anything that would give them that clue that had been eluding them from the start, the motive. It took most of the night, and by the time they were finished, the sun was starting to break through the curtains. "Nothing," said Ruff as he met up with the colonel.

"Likewise, my boy, this blighter's got us beat, eh, what," said the colonel jokingly.

Ruff and the colonel again headed back to the kitchen to pour out the coffee, Ruff sat down and handed the other coffee to colonel. "I have a motive. Someone is cultivating cannabis plants in Lady Pottersby's house and that is not right, she has been very kind and considerate."

As the sunshine came upon them again, the colonel began to think. "We searched every bit of Moontown and nothing; maybe the killer has left and taken his equipment with him?" said the colonel.

"That's just straw-grabbing," said Ruff. After a while and with no one credible coming forward, Ruff decided to return to where it began. Looking for help, Ruff sat at the table, waiting for the next person to come in. Then it happened, a refined-looking lady appeared and sat down across from him on the table. "Can I help you, love?" asked Ruff in the most refined voice he could muster.

"I think you need the help," she replied.

Ruff looked up from his scribbling only to see Helen staring at him. "You."

"What's the matter, I thought you wanted help?" asked Helen.

"Yes, I do, I mean we do, to catch a killer, but how can you help?" said Ruff.

"Did you not think that maybe I may have been at the party too," said Helen. Ruff pulled out his notepad and got ready to scribble down anything that he thought would be useful. "Well, let's start from the top," said Helen. "The thing is, Lady Pottersby knows me and she invited me as her guest along with about 99 others, who she also invited. Pretty close to one o'clock in the morning when the party was starting to die down, I saw a man, and he was acting rather strange. While others were dancing in the main ballroom, he was just staring as though either he did not know what to do or how to do it. Then for whatever reason, he left. Call it curiosity, but I remembered his face and about, I would say, 20 minutes later he came back, but this time he was arguing," said Helen.

"With whom?" asked Ruff.

"Jarvis, of course," said Helen.

Ruff looked stunned, why had Jarvis never mentioned this to him before. "Go on," he asked.

"Well, I got some of the argument but at its height there were raised voices, and I believe someone threw a punch," said Helen.

"Go on," said Ruff.

"Well, it was actually a silly argument about bugs, he claimed he had bugs all over him," said Helen, "but the odd thing is that when the punch was thrown, I know this as I heard someone hit the floor. After a while, the two people left the room, only—" said Helen.

"Only what?" asked Ruff.

"Whoever left the room was carrying the other one," said Helen.

At this point, Ruff was frantically scribbling away on his paper. *Was Jarvis involved in these murders and if so, how much did he know about the others? Whatever happens,* thought Ruff, *my next job is to find Jarvis and get him to explain.* As time pushed the day along, finding Jarvis was not the easiest of tasks, Ruff literally searched every inch of the house; where could he be? Finally, when Ruff had given up hope, Jarvis appeared from one of the rooms. "Eh up, love," said Ruff.

"Yes, sir," said Jarvis.

"We need to talk, love," said Ruff. Jarvis and Ruff headed back down to the kitchen and Ruff put the kettle on to prepare to find out what Jarvis really knew about the cannabis plants and everything else.

"So, what do you know?" asked Ruff.

"How do you mean, sir?" asked Jarvis.

"I've just had a long chat with Helen about things and she claims you had an argument with a man about some cannabis plants and some of the things that destroy them," said Ruff.

"Is that so?" said Jarvis.

"It is so, and you also should know that the cultivation of cannabis is illegal on Moontown and punishable by death," said Ruff.

"I do know, sir; that is why I have nothing to do with them," said Jarvis.

"Well, tell me what Helen was saying," asked Ruff.

"On the night of the party, I was talking to Walter Bens about cannabis plants, he said he had come up with a foolproof way of cultivating them so that no one found out," said Jarvis.

"How?" asked Ruff.

"Synthetic cannabis, it has the same effect, but the police cannot do anything as chemically they are different, so if—" said Jarvis.

"You were caught, technically you were breaking no laws as what you had cultivated chemically was not cannabis," finished Ruff.

"Yes," said Jarvis.

"So, what went wrong?" asked Ruff.

"Evelyn went wrong. Evelyn Trubshaw was at the college trying to get qualifications to get her out of her paper job so she could get something better in an office, the only problem was that Mr Puktar wanted her in bed. The other problem was Bens was giving out free samples and one person he had given it to was Puktar," said Jarvis.

"I fail to see it, love. If it is what you said, it's synthetic cannabis, you can't be tried," said Ruff.

"Like most things in life, it's a case of trial and error mostly the error," said Jarvis.

"How do you mean?" said Ruff.

"The sample that Puktar took was far too strong, it gave him the lot, shakes, paranoia, hallucinations," said Jarvis.

"So, you're saying that Puktar killed Evelyn?" said Ruff.

"That I don't know, but I would say it was a strong possibility, he was at the party but then again, so was Bens," said Jarvis.

"Is Bens the man you hit?" said Ruff.

"No, the man I hit was—" All of a sudden, Jarvis crashed face-first to the table with a thud, the back of his head destroyed by a close-range bullet, which did its job, leaving bits of Jarvis all over Ruff.

As you may have guessed, Ruff was not a fast man, but again sometimes situations make you do things that you never thought you could; this was the turn of Ruff, he moved very quickly to avoid whoever was shooting. Not long after, the colonel appeared, to be greeted by what was left of Jarvis arranged around the chair he was sat on. "What happened?" asked the colonel.

"He was in the middle of telling me who he hit when someone shot him," said Ruff.

The colonel went over to the window to look out, there was no apparent bullet hole which meant the bullet was probably still lodged in what was left in the skull of Jarvis.

It almost seemed like a regular road trip as the colonel and Ruff pulled up at the mortuary. "Good morning, my friends," welcomed the mortician, "my, you did send me a messy one. I've been up to my arms in Jarvis all morning," said Ralph.

"What did you find out?" asked Ruff.

"Well, it looks like a dum-dum bullet," said Ralph.

"What's that?" said Ruff.

"A dum-dum is a filthy thing; what they do is hollow out the end of the bullet and then fill it up with mercury, and then when it hits its target, it flattens on impact. It's called dum-dum because of the noise it makes when it hits the target," said the colonel.

"I don't think this was intentional, the bullet I mean, I just think he or she wanted to shut up Jarvis as he was about to tell you something which the killer feared may reveal his or her identity," said Ralph.

Ruff looked at the mortician. "I don't suppose you can help as I am very slowly slipping back to square one," pleaded Ruff.

The mortician looked at Ruff and then at the colonel. "This must be your lucky day, I do have something I can give you," said the mortician as he walked over to the body of the dead butler. Ruff braced himself for the sight that was about to befall him and was doubly relieved when it was only his hand. "See this green resin?" said the mortician holding out the hand of the dead man. Both Ruff and the colonel leaned over to have a look.

"It looks like pea soup or fag ash," said Ruff.

"It's cannabis resin, and I'll show you something else." The mortician revealed the veins on his arm. "He was mainlining," said Ralph showing the track marks running up his arm. Then Ralph lifted out the dead man's leg. "He was starting on those as well. Your friend was a user, heroin," said Ralph.

"Any idea where Walter Bens is?" Ruff asked Ralph.

"Not really but I had heard on the news that he was in prison. I don't think he's dead and as I'm the only game in town, he would have had to have come through here unless he died abroad. Even so, I reckon I would have seen him sooner or later," said Ralph.

Back to the car they headed one more time as the colonel turned on his engine. "Where are we going?" asked Ruff.

"To the prison. If we want any answers, we have to go to see him, he must know someone or something. I think we are getting close," said the colonel as he started the car.

"So, you think these murders are drug-related?" said Ruff.

"Maybe not," said the colonel, "my theory is that in the mansion that we are in now, someone is hiding something that no one wants found, and whoever it belongs to will keep killing until it is safe," said the colonel.

"So, it could be valuable?" said Ruff.

"Drugs; could be millions," said the colonel.

The car finally pulled up outside the prison. On the outside it looked like a giant castle, like Colditz, even currently it lacked the refinements of a modern-day prison. As the two men approached the forbidding gates, the weather started to change as a chill hit the air. As the bell was rung, a dull clang pierced the air and then footsteps as the gates that had obviously not been oiled for some time, swung open. "You might be?" said the guard.

"I might be Ruff and this is the colonel; Lady Pottersby sent us."

The guard examined his list, he was just about to deny entry when he saw their names at the bottom of the list. The two men walked into the prison and through the massive courtyard into a more modern-looking part with big bullet-proof plexiglass windows to, one would assume, protect the workers from possible random acts of violence. The two men were led into a room where the prisoner sits on one side and relatives on the other, the only difference is there were no relatives.

Finally, after waiting some time, he appeared, Walter Bens. He was about six foot three and he wore a prison-issue, orange coat with his name and number on it. Walter sat down, looking at Ruff staring at him. "Hello, Walter," said Ruff.

"What do you want?" asked Walter.

"We need information on a cannabis plant," said Ruff.

"I'm doing a ten-stretch in here, you are seriously asking me to buy drugs?" said Walter.

"No, we want your advice, we think there could be a cannabis factory at the old mansion where Lady Pottersby lives," said Ruff.

"So what?" said Walter.

"Someone is going around murdering everyone in their path until finally they are safe and secure, and we would like to save Miss Pottersby before it's too late," said the colonel.

"Miss Pottersby, eh?" said Walter as he stroked his chin wistfully. "She's a tough old bird, bit strange but does not deserve that."

"We kind of like her as well," said Ruff.

"So what? Has she hired you, are you PIs or what?" said Walter.

"I'm a builder by trade doing repairs to the house, she hired me to find the killer," said Ruff.

"Have you had any experience?" said Walter as he looked again at Ruff.

"Murder mystery weekend," said Ruff.

"So, what are you? Comic relief or does she really think you will find the killer?" said Walter.

"I have got some leads though," said Ruff.

"Really," said Walter.

"This is why we are here; our investigation has brought us to your office, we need your help before Lady Pottersby gets killed," said Ruff.

"Did you notice the insects in the roses?" said Walter.

"Yes, but that's not why we are here," said Ruff.

"Oh, I beg to differ, officer, you and I both want the killer caught, the only problem is, I never get the opportunity. You see, someone in the mansion has a cannabis plant but he wants it hiding so that when the police come looking, there will be nothing there to see."

"So, you are convinced it is a man," said Ruff.

"Indeed, in fact I can also say that I know who the killer is," said Walter.

Both Ruff and the colonel looked at each other. Finally, it was over, all that remained is for the killer to be picked up and then for Ruff and the colonel to go back to their day jobs. "Don't keep us in suspense, who is it and why?" said the colonel, in his own way kind of sad his adventure would soon be ended. Finally, Walter announced the name of the killer and the name was a surprise but not a shock.

"The killer is Mr Puktar, he was having an affair with a student and she made a tape," said Walter. Ruff walked forward and whispered in his ear.

"Mr Puktar is dead." He took a while to react, but finally emotion overcame him, and he started cheering.

"Excuse me, we have a dead body here and you're cheering, how can you be so callous?" said Ruff.

"I knew the man he was loathsome, he used to come to Lady Pottersby's parties, he would spend the first half getting high with the young girls, and the second half threatening the girls unless they obliged him sexually," said Walter.

Ruff and the colonel glanced at each other and with a quick nod of the head, they were off, back to the car and back to the warmth of the boiler in the kitchen and no one to answer to but themselves. They looked to see just where they were now as, once again, night was beginning to claw the air to black. As they drove back to the mansion's kitchens together, Ralph and the colonel began talking. "So, where does that leave us now?" asked Ruff.

"Well it proves that Puktar was a dirty old bastard who liked to fondle teenagers," said Ruff.

"A dead, dirty old blighter," repeated the colonel.

"It still doesn't help, though, as we can't put him in the frame as he is already dead," said Ruff.

"True," said the colonel, "but we can add him to the information we have received. Just out of interest, are you happy that we now have a killer of Evelyn and a few others?" said the colonel.

"No, I know people did not like Puktar, but I still can't place him at the crime, I need more time to think," said Ruff.

"I think it is only fair to give madam our weekly report, and I don't think turning around and saying we are actually moving backwards with our investigations would be very fortuitous to us continuing the case, do you?" said the colonel. Ruff thought for a second before answering.

"I'll tell you what, you tell her, and I'll stay in the background looking pretty. Agreed?" said Ruff.

"Agreed," said the colonel. The colonel went to see Lady Pottersby.

"Ah, Colonel, how goes the investigation?" said Lady Pottersby.

The colonel explained about how things were slowly but surely moving forwards, but as Lady Pottersby said, "The one suspect we have is now dead so where do we go from here?" And although he would not admit it, the colonel did not know either. As the night drew in, Ruff was getting ready to go to bed only to be greeted on the stairs by a very anxious Lady Pottersby.

"I do not wish to push you, Ruff, but do you think these murders will ever stop?" said Lady Pottersby.

Ruff thought for a moment; of course, as soon as the killer runs out of people to murder, but you cannot really say that to someone who has put their faith in you that you will find the killer and bring them to justice. "Well, Lady Pottersby, the way I see it is this," just as he reached the end of his sentence, the phone rang cutting him off.

"I'm sorry, my dear, with dear Jarvis no longer with us, I have to answer the phone myself," said Lady Pottersby.

"I can do it, love," said Ruff as he wobbled his enormous bulk to the phone. "Hello, Pottersby residence," said Ruff.

Lady Pottersby had made it to Ruff on the phone just in time to see him slowly drop it back on the cradle.

"What on earth is the matter?" she asked.

"There's been another one," said Ruff.

"Another murder, where?" she said.

"At the prison. Walter is dead," said Ruff, just in time for the colonel to appear. "Now we are back to square one," said Ruff.

Part Six

Hip Hip You Die

As they approached the prison, the ambulance had just turned up. Ruff and the colonel walked inside. "Come to see the body, love, Lady Pottersby sent us," said Ruff. As they approached the cell, they could tell a struggle had occurred, there was blood everywhere and what looked like bits of an ear that was missing. Ruff bent down to remove the sheet as a big roar went up.

"You show me that again and I'll arrest you," said the guard as Ruff lifted up his jeans. Pulling back the sheet, Ruff could already see that Walter's left ear had been partly mutilated, at least the top half had been, but apart from that his body appeared fine. So, what had made the blood and why was Walter dead? Surely the wound was not severe enough for him to die.

The colonel arrived on the scene not five minutes behind Ruff as he said he had been talking to the prison guard. "He said he heard a lot of commotion and found Walter lying on the floor with part of his ear missing but that was about it. He thinks it was not bad enough for someone to die, so there must have been—" said the colonel.

"A second person," finished Ruff. "This is definitely one for the mortuary, I can't perform an internal investigation no matter how much faith Lady Pottersby has in me," said Ruff.

As Ruff talked, two ambulancemen came in and took the body away, ready to take him down the mortuary, and once again, Ruff was left alone with his thoughts as a cold wind flew across the cell. Just as Ruff was about to leave, he noticed out of the corner of his eye a piece of paper tucked, but in such a way it would be noticed, under a pillow. Ruff looked around to make sure no one saw him then gingerly lifted up the pillow and removed the paper. Ruff looked down at the paper and to his surprise, it was a train time but no date. This was indeed confusing, thought Ruff, but the thing was, there was only one station in the whole of Moontown and although there was no date, he had a feeling that whatever was going to happen would happen today. Ruff tucked the note into his trouser pocket hoping that whatever this was would give him the lead he wanted so as he could start to make some real progress in this case.

Ruff left the cell and headed back to the colonel's car. "Find anything, old boy?" asked the colonel. Ruff handed him the crumpled-up piece of paper he had concealed in his trousers, the colonel read it. "This could be anything, it's just a train time, no station or anything," said the colonel.

"We have to, for once, assume it is this station," said Ruff. "The worst that happens is we hang around for a bit and catch cold, the best is we may meet someone who could finally put us on the right track," said Ruff.

The two men went to the train station to meet the two-thirty train. The train station was one of those old-fashioned, run-of-the-mill type open-platform stations, two tracks with a bridge crossing over; lord help anyone if it started to snow as there was definitely no protection from the elements. The two men waited on the platform for the next train to arrive as all they had was a piece of paper, they did not even have the name of the train. After about half an hour of waiting, they decided it was time to stop. Who or whatever was going to arrive had obviously heard about the accident to Walter and probably no longer felt safe; and if it was to do with the killer, I guess the safest place would have been at home rather than facing the unknown, especially if that unknown took the form of a killer. As the two men walked toward the exit, the tannoy announcer came on: 'The next train to arrive at platform one is the two-thirty train for Ruff Buttocks.' The two men stopped dead, had they heard right? This train was for them; was this the killer playing games with them and if so, should they play?

The train crunched its way to a stop as all the gears finally broke in unison. As the train stopped, the doors opened to reveal blackness. *How could this be?* thought Ruff. *Blackness in a train carriage when it is broad daylight outside?* Ruff shuffled toward the train doors and stuck his head in. "Eh up, love, anyone home?" said Ruff. The reply was not long in coming as Ruff felt himself being thrust forward with what felt like a pair of arms pushing him inside the carriage, soon to be followed by the colonel. The two men sat aboard the train in silence as it began to move, slowly at first and then it began to gather pace and speed.

"Welcome on board, my friends," said the voice. "It seems you have been chasing me since I started killing off your friends."

"Aye, love, we would like you to stop, no offence, it's just it is not very friendly whoever you are," said Ruff.

"Who do you think I am?" asked the voice.

Now it was the turn of the colonel to play the guessing game. "Well, we had a few theories and then the plant infestation threw us a bit, and now I can honestly say we do not have a clue," said the colonel.

There was silence as the train gathered speed and then finally it stopped dead as the voice spoke only to issue a chilling warning. "Your friends, or those other people, got too close, they had to die. I'm sorry, but believe me, it had to be done, too close they got," said the voice. Then again, there was a measured silence as if the voice was thinking its next move out.

"I am really sorry," said the voice, "but I am afraid now you two are too close, and as a result, you too must die. Goodbye." With that, the train began to hurtle forward at an alarming pace.

"Ere, love, what are you doing?" asked Ruff as the train carried on gathering speed but no matter how many times Ruff asked, there was no reply; whatever or whoever it was had left the train.

"We need to stop the blighter," said the colonel as he awoke in the kitchen. "What's going on, sir?" said the colonel as he was checking his surroundings again and again.

"What do you mean?" asked Ruff.

"We were on board a train, sir, it damn well nearly killed us," announced the colonel.

Ruff gave him a sideways glance. "You were, love, not me," said Ruff.

"How do you mean, sir?" asked the colonel.

"You were dreaming," said Ruff. The conversation between Ruff and the colonel went on for some time as Ruff started to wonder why the colonel had this dream.

Meanwhile, in the garden, Lady Pottersby was attending to her tulips and various other flowers. For the past four years in Moontown, no one had even come close to her ladyship in the form of flowers and flower-arranging. No one knew what it was, but she seemed to have the knack of laying the right flower at the right time and then later on a huge arrangement would spread across her borders. She was the envy of most people in the village of Moontown and beyond, as everyone knew, when it came to flowers, she was second to no one. As she attended her flowers, Lady Pottersby was always armed with the very latest in technology, even though she did not agree with such things, she knew that anything that made her life easier could only be a positive step in the right direction. When she had finished, she liked to walk along a line of them in turn, like a sergeant major marshalling his troops getting ready for the big parade, although as she knew, these flowers would never stand to attention, even for her. As she began her final walk past her prized blooms, she noticed that one of her roses was infected with what she believed was aphids, so grabbing a can of weed spray she let loose and then let out a scream. The colonel and Ruff heard this and bolted out the door into the garden in case the old lady was being attacked. Instead, the sight that greeted them was a much different one indeed as she was left dumbfounded, and pointing to one plant in particular, which had suddenly begun to melt. It was the ammonia, but did that mean that someone had it in for her ladyship and that indeed now she was a legitimate target for whoever was on their murderous rampage?

Ruff and the colonel carried the old lady back to the house and back upstairs to her bedroom and laid her out on her bed. After about five minutes, she woke up. "Where am I?" asked her ladyship.

"You're in your bed, love, I brought you back," said Ruff.

"Brought me back from where?" asked her ladyship.

Ruff explained how he had saved her after he heard the scream and saw the smoke rising from her best flowers, knowing full well, albeit accidentally, she had used the weed killer intended as it was to kill as it had been laced with ammonia. So, thought Ruff, it looked as though Lady Pottersby would indeed be the next target. Could he interview her? Maybe she could give the investigation new leads. The final thing, thought Ruff, what had she seen or stumbled across that now made her so dangerous that she had to be killed. So now, thought Ruff, detective to bodyguard.

Ruff decided maybe the next step was to go back to the mortuary, maybe he had something he could tell them. As Ruff and the colonel arrived, they were greeted by Ralph. "Good morning, gentlemen, and how may I assist you today?" he asked.

"We need to know more about the prison death, is there anything you can tell us?" the colonel asked.

"Well, it's unusual," said Ralph.

"In what way unusual?" said Ruff.

Ralph went into the back room and revealed the body in all its glory. "It was a normal death," he said. "Well, normal compared to the ones you usually bring me, he died of a heart attack," said Ralph.

The two men looked at each other before the colonel finally spoke. "Heart attack, eh, well the blighter, how did it happen?"

"How heart attacks normally happen; his arteries were totally furred up. I took out the heart and completely examined it, there were plaques but apart from that, nothing. I would say high cholesterol, maybe one too many cheeseburgers," said Ralph.

"So, nothing unusual about his death?" asked the colonel.

Ralph looked at him with a knowing glance. "Well, one odd thing."

"I knew it," said Ruff banging his hand on the table.

"The top of the ear had been eaten off," said Ralph.

"Eaten off?" said the colonel with surprise.

"Eaten off by thrips," said Ralph, "when they appear from the pupal stage, they are hungry and will eat anything."

"You mean someone put them there?" said the colonel.

"Yes, someone deliberately put them there, why, I could not possibly tell you," said Ralph.

The two men once again left the mortuary and got into the car. "Where now?" asked Ruff.

"The beach," said the colonel as he drove his car with purpose.

At the moment it was a lovely day as the colonel pulled his car up by the sandy dune cliffs and the two men got out. The colonel walked over to the cliff edge and proceeded to look over the edge at the sand below, there were many stones scattered over the beach and the sea was still a long way off. Ruff soon joined the colonel after he pulled himself out the car. "What are we looking for, love?" asked Ruff. The colonel paused for a moment and let out a small sigh before speaking.

"I think, sir, that we are close, so close, and I think also that if we do not find this killer soon, there will be a pile of dead bodies on our hands," said the colonel.

For the first time, Ruff looked exasperated. "What can I do, love? I'm a builder by trade, I'm fat, and my arse-crack is on display for all to see, beyond that, I'm pretty much useless," said Ruff.

The colonel turned and grabbed what he could of his huge bulk. "Don't say that, sir, remember that murder mystery weekend, you're a damn fine detective. You have done it once, now you can solve this; the only difference is that this is real, whereas the murder mystery weekend was just a test. Now, just think, did you win the weekend?" said the colonel.

"Well, yes, I guess, love, I mean I found the murderer, they actually said it was quite remarkable that I had unravelled the clues," said Ruff.

"Exactly, sir, now all I and Lady Pottersby want is for you to do it again, but this time in a real scenario and a real body," said the colonel.

Ruff thought about the words for a moment, was he right, could he really solve this case? "OK, love, I'll buy that, so what now?" asked Ruff.

The colonel looked away from Ruff and once again out to the sea as the weather was starting to become colder and the tide was starting to turn. "Let's go down onto the beach and we will have a walk, sir," said the colonel.

The two men finally found a path down to the beach through the masses and masses of sand dunes. But could there ever be a conclusion to this case? It seemed everyone they suspected was either dead or had disappeared, so where now? "So, we are missing some parts of the puzzle. Think of it like a jigsaw, you can't complete your jigsaw without the correct picture and then the correct pieces slotted into place. In that scenario, we have the right picture, but the pieces are all wrong," said the colonel. "We are missing something; our jigsaw lacks the correct pieces. Tell me this, if you have been given a building job to do and it was too complicated, I mean you get to the end of the instructions and you still have no idea of what to do, what do you do?" said the colonel.

Ruff thought about it for a moment. "I guess I would go back to the start and see what I had missed," said Ruff. At this point, the colonel gave a vice-like grip to Ruff.

"Exactly, my good fellow, we need to retrace our steps and see what we are missing, once we have our missing piece then perhaps we can start on our jigsaw," said the colonel. Ruff looked at him and then looked down at his feet and the footprints he was making in the sand. "We start with Evelyn Trubshaw, now what do we know about her?" said the colonel.

"Well," said Ruff, "everyone seemed to like her, and everyone seemed shocked at her murder, but we had a lead – Mr Puktar had made advances," said Ruff.

"Money motive?" asked the colonel.

"I would doubt it as she was just a girl making it in the paper shop," said Ruff.

"You forget one thing, Ruff, the tape. We assumed Puktar wanted it as it contained incriminating evidence, but maybe someone wanted it more?"

Ruff thought about this for a moment and also began to ponder. "So, we really need this tape, love?" said Ruff.

"I would agree, old boy, but remember, we do not know who has it; we assumed that Puktar had it, but he gets himself murdered by someone," said the colonel.

"The killer," added Ruff hopefully.

"Quite possibly," added the colonel. Ruff looked a bit disheartened, quite possibly, quite probably, thought Ruff. "So now the second murder, old boy," said the colonel, "Bertha Breasts. As the mortician informed us, all three were poisoned by this drug, we do not know what it is as yet but the killer likes to use it, let's assume all three were the same drug, we can assume that it was the same killer for all three," said the colonel.

"Why the hand job on Evelyn and why was Bertha mutilated?" said Ruff.

"Tell me, old boy, some people say cannabis can be good in small doses and it relieves arthritis and suchlike," said the colonel.

"Yes, I've heard it does," said Ruff.

The colonel looked at Ruff then away again. "It's bull, I took it for my arthritic shoulder, all I got was being chased by my dead ex-wife for the next three days." Ruff tried desperately to suppress his laugh. "It was awful, I was sat on the toilet and she sat on the bath next to me chattering whilst I was trying to go. Puts one off it does," said the colonel.

Ruff was nearly in tears of laughter. "So, your point is?" he sniggered. The colonel looked at him.

"Despite what they say, for some people, cannabis has the effect of making people paranoid. This is my theory, for what it is worth, he was so paranoid that he tried to destroy the bodies any way he could as he was concerned he would be identified. Remember what the mortician said? The decapitated body was a ragged scar. If you were thinking straight and decided to decapitate someone, what would you use?" said the colonel.

Ruff thought for a moment. "Well, I guess some sort of meat cleaver, clean cut, no mark, straight through everything," said Ruff.

"Exactly, old boy, now you're getting it. But he didn't; this person used an implement like a saw to make a rough, jagged incision, the time it must have taken him to remove her head, so much time that he was probably seconds away from being caught, whereas if he had used a meat cleaver, straight in and out," said the colonel.

"Which proves what?" said Ruff.

"Which proves this person, whoever it was, did not think straight, one of the major effects of paranoia," said the colonel, slowly but surely, a picture was starting to emerge in his head. "Onto the third murder, Mr Puktar; again, it was a very odd murder, it was made to look like suicide even though it never was, again paranoia but we have an added factor, one of the causes of death was strangulation and the other was poison. When I asked Ralph, he said the hyoid bone was broken in the neck, which is very hard to break and is also a significant post-mortem find, it suggests he was strangled," said the colonel.

"Suggests is not definite," said Ruff.

"He also had a petechial haemorrhage, which again shows signs of strangulation but yet he also was drugged," said the colonel.

Ruff started to think, and pulling out his notebook, he started to make his own notes. Ruff thought, *Does any of this make sense, I wonder?*

"What about Lucy; that was brutal," said Ruff.

"Lucy is the one odd one in this, but to tell you more we will have to go to the mortuary," said the colonel. Ruff thought for a moment.

"Why can't you tell me?" asked Ruff. The colonel never answered but simply rose to his feet and headed out of the door. It was becoming a habit this thought Ruff as the colonel's car headed back to the mortuary.

The two men left the car to be greeted by Ralph. "Back again so soon, gentlemen, next thing will be you will want me to solve the case for you and that I am afraid I cannot do," said Ralph.

"I would like you to explain to my friend here all about Lucy and how she met her end and why?"

Ralph looked at the colonel and started to speak. "Lucy was raped," said Ralph.

"Raped?" said Ruff. "She was only half-naked," concluded Ruff.

"This is something I must admit, as a coroner, has me stumped. I did the tests and we got a semen sample, and she was definitely raped."

"I am sorry," said Ruff. "On the plus side, if we can match up the semen sample to the body, we have the killer," said Ruff.

The colonel and Ralph looked at each other and both looked very confused. "We have matched it up," said the colonel.

"Great, so we now have a solid lead; let's get him, who does it belong to?" said Ruff.

Ralph walked over to his desk and pulled out a sheet of paper with a list of names and one of the names had been circled with a red pen. Ruff looked at the sheet. "Harry Queets. So, what is the problem? Let's go arrest him, Lady Pottersby can get us a warrant," said Ruff.

The colonel looked at Ruff then at Ralph. "We know exactly where he is and getting a warrant will not be an issue. In fact, arresting him will not be a problem as he will not put up a fight."

"Great," said Ruff, let's go." The colonel looked at Ruff.

"The man is already dead," said the colonel.

Ruff looked at Ralph and then back at the colonel. "How can he be dead? You're saying she was raped by a dead man?" said Ruff.

"That is exactly what I am saying, we checked and double-checked and it's definitely correct. She was raped by a dead man and we can only assume the dead man removed her breasts", said Ruff

"So, what happens now?" asked Ruff.

The colonel pondered, and Ralph came up quickly with a solution. "In Moontown, there is a law that states a body can never be exhumed, it does work into the hands of murderers, but we here in Moontown believe in the principle of rest in peace; once the coffin lid is nailed down, it stays down," said Ralph.

Suddenly Ruff started to look very worried. "I hope you're not suggesting what I think you are," said Ruff.

The colonel decided to remove all doubt. "We need to check, old boy; we need that body."

Ruff looked as though he was about to vomit all over the floor, his face began to turn green and his pulse started to race, and a faintness started to envelop his body. In the end, the feeling of nausea became so much that he could not take it anymore and his huge frame wobbled into a chair tucked into the corner. "Look, love, I would love to solve this case, I would even love to be called detective of the year, but I draw the line at stealing bodies, there is no way I am doing this, no way no how, I am a building worker, not a grave robber," said Ruff.

"Also, what is the penalty for grave robbing if we are caught?" said Ruff. Again, the colonel and Ralph looked at each other.

"I think we could get Lady Pottersby to, how shall we say, *divert* the police while we look for the body," said the colonel.

Ruff looked for a moment as though perhaps he would agree to this bizarre plan if indeed he was backed into a corner. "Is there no other way?" enquired Ruff.

"No other way," said the colonel. "I am a great war hero, if I was caught can you imagine what would happen to me, can you imagine what people would say?" Ruff turned around and looked at the colonel.

"Me as well, maybe I am not as important as you, but I still do have a lot to lose if I am caught and also what will you be doing, love, while we are under the ground fiddling with the coffin?" said Ruff with some panic in his voice.

"As you know, you are taking a risk, but once the body is safely here in the mortuary, I can just claim I found it in the street, and it would be almost impossible to prove that I was actually lying if anybody felt like challenging me."

Ruff started to think about everything. He knew perfectly well what he was risking by going ahead with this bizarre scheme, but on the other hand if he refused, he may never find the truth behind this mystery and also the colonel would be with him to help. After a while, Ruff gave in, "OK, love, I'll do it," said Ruff with his voice full of uncertainty.

"So, how do we do this?" asked the colonel.

"As soon as possible," said Ralph, "the sooner the body is here, the sooner I can examine the body and maybe give you the answers you are looking for."

The colonel and Ruff left the mortuary and headed back to the mansion to get prepared. The time soon disappeared and before they knew what was happening, it was 11 o'clock, and it was time. The two men started to prepare with shovels and all the digging equipment they needed when Lady Pottersby suddenly entered. "Well, gentlemen," she said with a refined air to her voice, "I hope you know what you are doing as I can only hold the police for so long, and as I am sure Ralph said, if anything was to happen to you two and you were caught, I cannot get involved because of my position. So, you are on your own, and you also know what the penalty is, don't you?" she said. Ruff looked at her and spoke.

"This may surprise you, love, but I want nothing at all to do with this scheme. I do not mind interviewing people, I do not even mind travelling, but I draw the line at grave robbing. However, I did say that I would help you and one way or the other, I will see this through to the end."

At this point, Lady Pottersby put her arms around Ruff and hugged him as best as someone could hug a man of his great size. "You do realise that if you can pull this off, you will be nothing short of famous," said Lady Pottersby.

Ruff looked at her as he laced up his boots. "Yes, the other situation is, if I do not pull this off, myself and the colonel are staring at an almost certain death sentence," said Ruff.

The colonel decided it was time for him to interject something into the conversation, which hopefully might give Ruff some more confidence in what he was about to face. "In the war, don't you know, we had to shift bodies all the time what, it's speed that we need," said the colonel. The two men continued to get ready as Lady Pottersby started to make some phone calls to people she knew. About half an hour later, she reappeared back in the kitchen to see the two men, almost unrecognisable, completely dressed in black, looking like a couple of commandos.

Lady Pottersby sat down at the table in the kitchen and told the two men exactly what she had done to help them.

"OK, gentlemen, I have kept the police diverted for the next two hours, after that, they may descend on the graveyard, and when they do, it will be very quick. Do not worry about driving at speed, as I said, I have diverted the police for two hours, so my advice to you would be to get in and out as quickly as you can. Get the body and get it back to Ralph, then your involvement ends, then it is just a case of coming back here and waiting to find out what has happened. Good luck."

Lady Pottersby shook the hands of the two men as she realised that this may be the last time she would see them, at least free anyway. The two men rose to their feet and got ready to leave when Ruff turned around and looked at Lady Pottersby. "If we do get caught, is there any chance that maybe you may be able to help?" said Ruff.

"All I can do is try, but hopefully that scenario is not going to happen." Lady Pottersby walked off, and Ruff and the colonel headed toward the driveway where the pickup truck was parked, filled to the brim with everything you could imagine, shovels and buckets and picks, everything a person could ask for.

"Good luck," said the colonel and he shook Ruff's hand as the two men entered the pickup truck for what would perhaps be the most dangerous part of this investigation.

With hearts full of hope, the old man and the young man were ready to set off together as finally they turned on the engine and headed toward the graveyard. After a short while, the pickup truck stopped by the cemetery gates as Ruff got out and opened them. There was a big lock on the gates, but Ruff took the bolt cutters out the back of the truck and with one swift move, the lock snapped, and the chain fell to the floor as the metal gates creaked open. Ruff walked over and pushed the gates the rest of the way as the pickup truck entered all the way. Ruff closed the gates and got back into the truck but not before flinging the bolt cutters into the back of the truck. The truck slowly made its way on the very dimly lit path all the way through the cemetery to its destination. Inside the truck, Ruff asked the obvious question. "Do you know where this grave is?" asked Ruff.

The colonel took his eyes off the road for a second and turned to Ruff. "Ralph came down here during the day to scout out the area and he has told me roughly where the grave is. We also have a large heavy-duty torch to help us with the light. Anyway, we have got two hours to find it," said the colonel as the truck ploughed on. Eventually, the truck arrived at its destination, and the colonel switched off the engine as the truck spluttered to a stop.

"Is this it?" enquired Ruff. The colonel never spoke but simply got out of the truck and went around the back, picking up the torch. After grabbing hold of it, the colonel shone on the grave, lighting up the name of Harry Queets. Suddenly a chill shot down the spine of Ruff as though he now knew what needed to be done but finally reality had hit him, and now the hard work began.

"Right, let's grab the shovel and get on with it," said the colonel. The two men grabbed the gear from the pickup truck and began to dig down into the ground. As the two men dug further and further, the area became harder to see as the light from the miner's lamp became more distant and dim to the point that the visibility became almost non-existent.

"You are going to have to grab the lamp and bring it down here," said Ruff wiping the sweat from his brow, realising that exhuming a body would be quite some task for a very fit man but for someone of Ruff's size and weight it was more than twice the task.

The colonel grabbed hold of the lamp and took it down to Ruff. The lamp lit up the working area, Ruff was covered in sweat and soil as the colonel arrived with the lamp. As the lamp arrived, the heat from it was making Ruff sweat even more. Not so close, thought Ruff as he kept digging further and further down into the ground until he finally hit something hard. Ruff handed the shovel to the colonel as the colonel handed him the pickaxe, what they had hit was no longer soil, it felt like clay. After a few wild swings with the axe, it was back to the shovel until finally they hit the box. Ruff looked up and started to scrabble out of the hole as the colonel was not far behind. As the two men finally made it out of the hole, they both looked down at the decayed wooden box and began to think how on earth were they going to bring this to the surface? The two men looked at each other and then down at the box and then again at each other and then one final look at the box. *Ropes*, thought Ruff, *wrap the ropes around and we can drag it to the surface.* Ruff went back to the bags they had brought with them and threw them down into the hole.

"You're going to have to go down there, love, I can't," Ruff said to the colonel. The colonel was not a young man and asking him to descend into a hole was not exactly the easiest of tasks. The elderly man gingerly descended into the hole until finally he was on top of the coffin. The colonel grabbed hold of the rope and started to unravel it as he started to secure the coffin, finally it was ready to be raised to the surface. The colonel struggled back to the surface with the help of Ruff. The two men started to pull the coffin to the surface, with much puffing and panting the coffin finally had been raised to the surface.

"So now all we must do is get it back to the mortuary." The colonel got into the car and backed it into Ruff as he swung open the doors and with the help of the colonel, he loaded the coffin into the back of the truck, locking the doors and securing it in place. The two men got inside the truck and began to drive back to the mortuary.

"This was a lot easier than I thought," said Ruff.

"Let's get this coffin back to the mortuary," said the colonel as the two men started to drive away. Fortunately for Ruff, the mortuary was not too far away, so the journey was not too long and after a short while, the car arrived and pulled up slowly by the mortuary office. Ruff got out of his seat and wobbled over to the door pressing the bell.

After a short while, Ralph appeared at the door. "Round the back," he whispered as he shut the door in Ruff's face. The two men took the coffin around the back of the mortuary only to be greeted by Ralph waiting with a trolley. The men loaded the coffin onto the trolley as it went inside. Ralph wheeled the coffin down the hallway and into the main room in the mortuary and Ralph got ready to do the post-mortem.

Ralph found himself a hammer and a chisel, and with the help of the colonel, they started to hit the coffin and gently break away the rusted nails. After what seemed like an eternity, it appeared as though all of the nails had finally been removed from the coffin and now all that was left to do was to lift open the lid. With the assistance of the colonel, Ralph started to pull open the box, leaving Ruff to look a bit queasy. "If you can't stomach it, old boy," said the colonel as Ruff left the room clutching his mouth to stop himself from being sick all over the floor. Back in the room, the two men kept pulling back on the lid until the whole body was exposed. To the surprise of Ralph, his body was very well preserved, it almost looked as though he had died only a couple of days ago, but of course this was not the case. So now the focus of the case had shifted, it was now totally in the hands of Ralph and the results of his investigations as to how this case was going to proceed. The colonel headed back outside into the cold night air as he saw his friend looking very unwell. "Not got the stomach, have you, old boy?" said the colonel.

"It was the smell, love, that's what got to me," said Ruff still looking very off-colour and still holding his mouth, it looked as though he had not been sick might be at any moment. The colonel got into the driving seat and it was not long before Ruff entered into the other side as his immense weight caused the truck to lean on one side. Ruff closed the door as the engine spluttered into life, and once again the two men were headed back to Lady Pottersby and her mansion.

When they finally arrived back, Lady Pottersby was waiting in the kitchen and hoping for some good news. The two men explained exactly what had happened and how they hoped things would go from now on, but what they hoped and what was going to happen could have been very different indeed. It had been a very tiring day for Ruff, for the colonel as well but mostly for Ruff as his stock-in-trade was as a builder and not as a detective. As a boy, Ruff often imagined himself as a hero, someone famous who one day everyone would know and respect but as a builder, the opportunities were just not there for him to fulfil his dreams. But now, as if by magic, life had presented him with a second opportunity to live his dream. Unfortunately for Ruff, things never went smoothly, and he was starting to realise that if he was indeed going to see his dream become reality, there was much more work to do. A tired Ruff finally climbed the mountain of stairs holding onto the magnificent golden bannister that snaked from downstairs to come to rest finally on the upstairs landing. Ruff approached his bedroom door and turned the door handle, his weary body entered the dark room as his hand groped for the switch. A cold breeze was kissing against his rugged features as he eventually found the dial and turned it, so the room was lit. The first thing Ruff noticed when he entered the room was that someone had opened his window, he remembered this as it had been a cold night and he made a point of closing the window so it would be nice and warm for when he returned. *To be honest*, thought Ruff, *I am not bothered* as he walked over to pull it shut. The huge man turned his enormous frame around and looked at his king-size bed with the crisp white sheets waiting for him, just as he had left it. With the murder of Lucy, there was no one now to do the bedrooms unless Lady Pottersby fancied having a go. But she was probably too old or unless she hired someone and the way she felt about outsiders coming in, both scenarios seemed an unlikely prospect. Ruff then let out a little chuckle to himself as he thought about the colonel, standing there in his pinny with a feather duster cursing the blighters. As Ruff approached his bed, he got hold of the top sheet and was just about to pull it back when he thought, *do you know what, this bed isn't half bad, I had better make sure that I am not next in line to be the chambermaid*; Ruff the detective he could handle but Ruff the chambermaid was too much even for him to consider.

Ruff finally pulled back the sheets and dropped his clothes to the floor as he grabbed his pyjamas and slid them over his huge bulk, first the bottom and then the top; he always did the bottoms first as he had trouble putting on the bottom half because of his waist. Suddenly the silence was broken by a scream piercing the air. *Bugger it,* he thought as he had just managed to lie down and standing up was no easy task when you were Ruff. He wobbled a bit to the left and then to the right as his enormous bulk was finally up. As fast as he could, Ruff slid on his trousers and with what air he had left in his body, he struggled for the door handle, opening it and going out into the dimly lit hall. It was late, very late, how late he did not care, he just wanted to locate the source of the screaming. It did not take him long as the screaming was constant. Eventually, as he got closer, he realised he was heading to the main chamber of Lady Pottersby. He entered the room at the very least expecting to see a dead body or two, but what he saw was probably more alarming, it was Lady Pottersby in her night things. *I am sure this is not what the old lady wanted me to see* thought Ruff. "Sorry to burst in, love, but I heard the screams," he said.

Lady Pottersby never spoke but just sat up in her bed shaking, she appeared to be holding a piece of paper. *What is it?* thought Ruff.

He approached the old lady and gently picked the piece of paper out of her hand. On it was written the words, Hip hip you die. *What does it mean?* thought Ruff.

At that moment, the colonel burst in. "What the bally hell is going on?" he exclaimed. On that note, Ruff extended his hand toward the old man, presenting him with the scrap of paper. Quickly reading it, he turned to Ruff and then to the old lady. "Probably someone's idea of a joke, who would say such a thing and what does it mean anyway?" said the colonel.

Ruff pondered for a moment and thought, *Is it a joke?* "I think the best thing, love, is for you to get some rest, I'm just down the hall if you need me," said Ruff as he grabbed the sheets and put the old lady back to bed. Ruff walked back toward the door and started to leave with the colonel when another scream rang out.

Ruff turned. "No, leave the light on, please," she announced.

"All right, love, if that's what you want," said Ruff walking out with the colonel and making sure she had plenty of light. Instead of heading back to bed, Ruff leant over to the colonel and whispered, "I think we should go to the kitchen and talk."

"Why the kitchen, why not the living room? I'll pour us a couple of brandies and well get a roaring fire going, eh what," said the colonel.

The two men walked down the stairs. In truth, the colonel walked down the stairs with Ruff following as Ruff had never been in the living room before as he did not feel right; after all, he was just a domestic and this was royalty. Finally, the two men arrived at two huge, wooden double doors, the frame encased in gold in the shape of two dragons, the tails wrapping around and the end of the tails forming the two door handles. The colonel grabbed the handles and pushed the doors opened. The room was in darkness until the colonel turned the light on. The sight that met Ruff next was one of immense splendour, it was a sight he never imagined he would see in his life as a building worker. The room was immense, it was almost like three rooms in one, at the far end was a magnificent mantelpiece, the top made of marble with a gold clock sat in the middle, just above was a full-length gold mirror. Along the sides of the room were huge windows, they must have been about ten-foot-high, like most other things in the house, the outer parts of the windows were again cased in gold. Into the middle of the room was a huge television, just off to the corner and in the middle was a huge leather settee and two big armchairs, the kind you sit in and keep sinking until you feel like you are about to drown. The carpet for some reason was bright red with a huge deep plush pile to it, walking in your bare feet was something you had to experience. In the other corner opposite the television was the drinks cabinet, it stood about five foot tall with every kind of drink you could imagine in it from brandy to lager to beer; you name it, the old lady had it in her drinks cabinet, if she didn't you could be sure, it was because she had run out of it.

"Sit down, old boy," announced the colonel. *Sit down,* thought Ruff, *where?* He looked around, and he felt out of place sitting anywhere, he almost felt that for courtesy's sake, he probably would be better off sitting on the floor. In the end, after searching for a couple of minutes, he decided the safest place would be one of the huge armchairs. Ruff walked over and sat down in the armchair and the leather sucked him in until you could barely make out his huge frame, for any kind of furniture to do that was indeed something out of the ordinary. Ruff used his strength to extricate himself from the leather that was trying to swallow him whole as he finally hauled himself up and regained his dignity. Strangely enough, as the colonel handed Ruff his brandy and sat down, Ruff noticed the colonel could sit down without being swallowed up by the chair. Ruff swilled the brandy in the glass before taking a sip, the mixture burning his lips. Ruff hadn't drunk brandy for some time as he was more of a beer down the pub with his friends sort of man, whereas he suspected the colonel was more of a three gin and tonics down the country club sort of man – after he had bagged a brace of pheasant of course. Ruff looked at the colonel without speaking, waiting and desperately hoping for him to be the one who would break the silence. For once, Ruff had no thoughts and absolutely nothing to say. *Hip hip you die,* thought Ruff, *what does it even mean?*

"Hip hip you die, old boy," said the colonel in a relaxed but refined voice, "any ideas?"

Ruff thought for a moment. *Is this the time for an intelligent answer or a constructive one?* Ruff thought. At the orphanage, they always said if in doubt, try for an intelligent answer.

"Maybe it is referring to something, people often say hip hip hooray, but not that," said Ruff.

"You're thinking too literally, old boy," said the colonel sloshing his drink in the glass, "I have a theory, any idea what hip might be referring to if it is something?"

Ruff tried hard to think but struggled to come up with an intelligent or indeed a constructive answer. After a while, the colonel put him out of his misery. "I think, old boy, that hip refers to rose hip the flower, the 'Hip hip you die' simply means poisoned rose hips. Lady Pottersby loves flowers," said the colonel.

"So, this murder and everything that has happened has been a plot to get rid of Lady Pottersby?" said Ruff.

The colonel sat across the room with a wry smile starting to stretch across his face. "What brings you to that conclusion, old boy?"

Again, Ruff looked as though he had run out of answers, and he was hoping someone was going to provide the missing information that he needed. "I just thought after what you said," said Ruff.

Again the colonel would not speak, he just smiled as though he was analysing his friend the way a psychologist might do if he was finding out if someone really was what he appeared to be or whether he was just faking it. "You want my opinion?" he said.

"Yes," said Ruff hoping that this might be the break he was looking for.

"I think that something is going on in this mansion, something downright illegal and I just think people are in the way," he announced.

"What about the murders?" said Ruff.

"I think the murders are a series of eliminations. Whoever is doing this, or indeed carrying them out, is doing it to remove the people who are in the way. Once all the people are gone, then they can continue with whatever they have planned," said the colonel."

Ruff thought for a moment before he spoke. "What, all the murders?" said Ruff.

"I think the next person in the way of the murderer is Lady Pottersby and I think she will be murdered or at least they will try," said the colonel.

Ruff thought about it for a moment, Lady Pottersby was very powerful with her connections but was she really a threat to anyone and what about the body they had just exhumed, ah yes, the body thought Ruff, where does that fit in. "The body in the mortuary, where does that fit in, assuming that your theory is correct?"

"The man in the mortuary committed rape to the girl who worked here, or at least someone framed him. When that party happened, there were about 100 guests here, I don't know how many we have interviewed but what I do know is, in my opinion, old boy, one of them holds the answer to this mess and one of them is the murderer." At this point, Ruff suddenly became very interested.

"You think you know the killer?" said Ruff.

"Oh no, old boy, that's your job finding the blighter, I am just trying to narrow it down for you. Do I know who the killer is? No. Do I know a motive? No, but I am starting to see one. I think you need to start the interviews again but now until we get the mortuary results, if it comes back the way I suspect it will, I think you may have a clear lead as to who did it. I think it is one of Lady Pottersby's guests simply because of the kind of lady she is. She has a very close circle of friends and staff, she does not just choose staff carefully, she chooses staff methodically." said the colonel.

"How so?" said Ruff.

The colonel looked at Ruff then looked away before finally looking back at him again. "Think about it, old boy, the girl is rolling in money, she could buy and sell most people on this planet many times over, she could afford to hire the greatest detectives in the world, but she has chosen you. No offence, old boy, she has chosen you because, like it or not, you are now part of her close circle of trusted friends. If she hires you to do a job, you can rest assured, she trusts you with her life," said the colonel.

Ruff looked at him and started to think about Lady Pottersby; the more he thought about the old lady, the more he realised he owed her a great debt even if the debt was simply one of trust. "So, what do I do now?" asked Ruff.

Again, the colonel looked at Ruff finishing his brandy. "That, my good man, I cannot tell you. You are the detective, like it or not, her ladyship hired you to find the killer, I will guide you as much as I can, but I can't tell you what you want to know. If I knew the killer, please believe me, I would tell you, old boy, but like you, all I have is theories. The blighter in the mortuary probably has nothing to do with it, maybe he just fancied getting fresh with the maid, only time will tell," finished the colonel.

Ruff finally looked exhausted. Was this the end of the line? It seemed to him as though the colonel knew how this was going to end and was withholding vital information from Ruff. Why? To make him look stupid? No, thought Ruff, I don't believe that. Well if it wasn't that then maybe he was telling the truth, maybe all the colonel had was, like Ruff, just theories. Once again, they were back at square one as the colonel rose. "I think it is bedtime for us both, the sun will soon be rising," said the colonel as he stretched his arms.

Ruff put down his brandy glass on the table next to him and proceeded to try and stand, his arms rhythmically flapping around like someone who could not swim frantically splashing for dear life. The colonel looked and gave a little laugh under his breath as he extended his hand to help Ruff to his feet. As the two men walked to the door, a huge bang sounded, shaking the building to its foundations, but was it a gun? Ruff looked at the colonel. "Not again," said Ruff.

"That was a door, old boy, I'm sure of it, I know a gun sound, and that was a door," said the colonel. The two men wandered around in the hall trying to locate where the noise had come from, but they did not have long to wait. As they turned the corner, Ruff noticed a half-opened door reflected in the moonlight with something apparently wedged in it. As he approached, Ruff's worst fears were confirmed, it was a human head.

As the colonel appeared, he too saw the sight, and then Lady Pottersby appeared from upstairs. "I heard a commotion," she announced as she covered her mouth to gasp as she saw what Ruff and the colonel were looking down at. Eventually, the two men got the door fully open for the head and the rest of the body to finally be in full view.

Ruff stepped over the body and turned on the light. Lying on the ground was a man about 50 years old with brown hair but with grey roots, his face was a mottled grey, his mouth was stuffed with red-orange-coloured rose hips and a note pinned to his chest. Ruff leaned over and unpinned the note which read Hip hip you die. Lady Pottersby looked down at the body, and it was indeed another one of her party guests. "This is Shaun Mayors."

Part Seven

A Dark Shadow

The first question Ruff asked was, who was Shaun Mayors? Lady Pottersby was not straightforward with the answer as she herself did not know a great deal about him. From what she said, there were suspicions that perhaps he may have been a drug dealer. If this was true, thought Ruff, it ties in nicely with everything else. It was starting to look, thought Ruff, as though everything that had happened so far was drug-related but if this was the case, what was the man doing dead? Ruff decided he needed to have a more in-depth talk to Lady Pottersby, but would she allow it? And also, how could he ask when he was just a glorified handyman? But then, she had hired him to find the killer, and if he was going to do this, Lady Pottersby was going to help him. Ruff called over Lady Pottersby and asked if he could talk to her. Lady Pottersby and Ruff went to her bedroom, and she sat on the bed as Ruff began his questions.

Ruff and Lady Pottersby started to talk, and they kept talking for hours and hours. Ruff was sure that she had the answers that perhaps would bring him the clarity he needed, after all, someone was hiding the information he needed. After talking to Lady Pottersby, Ruff did not feel a great deal better, what his long talk to Lady Pottersby told him was that he indeed did have the correct information; his problem was that perhaps there was someone he needed to talk to, but as yet, he had for one reason or another escaped Ruff's questions. *So, who is it?* thought Ruff. After talking to Lady Pottersby, he got up and walked over to the drawer in the kitchen and pulled out his long sheet of paper with a list of names on about a mile long. Perusing the list, Ruff was starting to realise that most of the people on his list had a red tick by them, which meant they had been interviewed and cleared or they were worthy of a second interview. One of these people was Sandra Stokes, she was a dowager and she lived in a stately home up the road. It was nowhere near as impressive a house as this; few houses in Moontown came up to this, even though Lady Pottersby kept her staff down to a select few, she still managed a steady, clean house. Ruff approached Lady Pottersby and asked about the dowager as she was at the party but was told by Lady Pottersby that she would be less than cooperative and her husband had a very bad temper, especially when common people were involved. Sandra Stokes, thought Ruff, looking at a picture Lady Pottersby had in the house. She was someone who Lady Pottersby had remarked she was not overly keen on, and she had even less time for her husband. Although Lady Pottersby was indeed wealthy and had many titles and royal connections, she treated everyone as equal. Ruff once again approached Lady Pottersby and reluctantly she made contact with the dowager who agreed to see Ruff, but in her house and not in Lady Pottersby's mansion.

Sunlight rose once again on Moontown as a chill air cascaded in through the open window. Would this be the day, thought Ruff, that the pieces he had would finally slot into place? Would this be the day that Lady Pottersby would be the glue that brought it all together by allowing the interview with Sandra Stokes? But what of the husband? Ruff was no stranger to a fist-fight, but it was not something he wanted to do unless it was in a pub in the name of fun. Ruff got dressed and had his breakfast and rose from the table, his enormous stomach smashing against the edge of the table. "Are you going?" asked Lady Pottersby.

"Yes, love," said Ruff, "just off to get the bike, it's a long ride." Lady Pottersby looked at Ruff and then walked over to the wall, unhooking a set of keys and handing them to the burly labourer. "What's this, love?" enquired Ruff as he looked down into the palm of his hand.

"I want you to take the convertible in the garage," she said.

Ruff looked both pleased and at the same time bemused. "The convertible, love?" questioned Ruff.

Lady Pottersby looked at Ruff, and she could see quite clearly he did not comprehend what was being asked of him. "You are going to see a very powerful lady, who I have no doubt will treat you like something off the sole of her shoe, but we need your mind in the right place. You take the convertible, you say you're an eccentric millionaire who has agreed to help out, under no circumstances tell her who you really are," said Lady Pottersby.

Ruff looked at her ladyship and down at the keys and then back at her before finally speaking. "I'm proud to be a labourer, love," said Ruff indignantly.

"I know you are, my good man, but for once trust me. I have no wish to see you get embarrassed and, believe me, as soon as she knows who you really are, you will not ask any questions, you will get *what's it like to work as a labourer* all afternoon, and her husband will probably be worse," she announced.

Again, Ruff looked at the keys and at her ladyship before finally bowing and saying thanks. Ruff left the room and headed down in the lift to the underground garage where her ladyship kept loads of cars, which one would suspect belong to someone else as in all the time here, Ruff had never seen her drive anywhere. As the lift stopped and the doors finally opened, Ruff extended his arm and did a clicking motion with the key; finally two lights flashed on a green convertible followed by a high-pitched squeak. Ruff walked over to the vehicle with a sense of anticipation, which soon turned to awe as he looked down at the giant motor. The convertible was a long, green two-seater with a black flattop foldaway roof. It was a very sleek design with lights to match and a racing stripe, and in the back, one rather large exhaust. Ruff opened the tiny door handle with his huge sausage fingers as he fumbled to click the glove compartment open; finally, it floated down. Ruff was about to close it when he noticed some papers had floated to the floor, presumably from the glove compartment. *What is yours is yours,* thought Ruff, but he quickly took a sneak peek while no one was looking, after all this may save him a journey. Ruff stuffed the papers back in, all except the last one which claimed a meeting with Shaun Mayors 2.15pm and a request 'bring white lightning'. *Was this a drug?* thought Ruff. Instead of putting it back inside, the burly man stuffed the now crumpled paper back in his top pocket.

Ruff put the keys in the ignition and turned on the car as the engine fired up with a loud roaring sound. Ruff was just about to reverse when his conscience started to prick him, he decided that his first visit must be to Ralph, maybe he had finished the post-mortem, and maybe he knew of white lightning. Ruff reversed out and gently pressed the accelerator and the car shot off down the driveway leaving Ruff barely in control. After what seemed like a matter of seconds, but in reality was much longer, the car found its destination as he screeched to a halt outside the mortuary. Ruff opened the door and walked toward the entrance to see a note attached on the inside: *Gone out,* it read, *back soon.* Oh well, thought Ruff as he turned back and headed to the green sports car. "Can I help you, love?" said the voice as Ruff turned, only to see Ralph and the colonel standing there. Ruff looked puzzled. "Sorry, just playing with you, love impersonations," said Ralph.

"Just came to look at progress, old boy, still need more time I think to blag this blighter," said the colonel.

Ruff reached into his top pocket and pulled out the crumpled paper. "Any ideas?" he asked as he handed the paper to Ralph.

The mortician took the paper from Ruff's outstretched hand and read it. "I can tell you about white lightning," said Ralph.

"Tell me, love," said Ruff.

"It is called cathinones; they have many names, white lightning is just one, it's similar to cocaine, people swallow, snort, smoke or inject it," said Ralph.

"What does it do?" asked Ruff looking at Ralph.

"Marijuana causes hallucinations, so does white lightning but it also causes paranoia, increased friendliness, increased sex drive, panic attacks, excited delirium, extreme agitation and violent behaviour," said Ralph, "naturally, it is banned on Moontown."

"I get the feeling there is a 'but' in your sentence," said Ruff.

"But it does not stop people getting it; literally any drug is possible to find if you really want it," said Ralph.

"So, could all these murders be drug-related, someone is trying to protect their stash?" said Ruff.

"It's a bold theory, old boy, but I am afraid you will have to back it up with hard evidence, you cannot just accuse people. Do you realise the penalty for what you are suggesting?" said the colonel.

"Most of these people are the royals or the elite, love," said Ruff, "if they were doing it, they would find a way to disguise what they were doing." The colonel looked at Ruff without breaking his gaze, and suddenly his expression turned to one of concern. For who? Ruff was not sure.

"Do you have a lead or someone in mind you want to talk to?" said the colonel.

"Sandra Stokes," announced Ruff.

The colonel looked at Ruff to make sure that this was indeed not a joke and he did indeed mean what he was saying. "Well, this should be fun, I really should have guessed. Is that the reason for the green car?" asked the colonel.

"I'm playing the eccentric millionaire, love," said Ruff.

The colonel looked at him. "Very eccentric," he said as he climbed into the car. "Any idea on a timeframe, old boy?" said the colonel to Ralph.

"The results should be in by tonight," said Ralph.

Ruff sat down on the leather seat and started the engine. "Next stop Sandra Stokes," said Ruff.

"Dowager Stokes," said the colonel. "I see you're going to need some advice on etiquette," said the colonel as the car fired off down the road. The car sped toward its destination as the two men chatted about so much, hoping to pool together what they had found and hopefully start to bring together the pieces of information that they did have like a sewing pattern or a jigsaw puzzle – no, no, a sewing pattern, yes, with each piece of the puzzle a stitch and finally, hopefully, they were coming together to give a clearer picture of who was behind these horrible murders thought Ruff. The car shot through the countryside at top speed as no one bothered about speed limits in Moontown, someone complained, you simply ran them down, no more person, no more complaint, except animals, even running over a cat, accident or no accident was punishable by death and you would surely die unless you possessed such money or contacts as you could buy yourself the best defence lawyers in the land. The air suddenly started to become thicker and it became harder to breathe as plumes of smoke filled the air. At first, Ruff thought it was a fire, but the colonel pointed out it was indeed a fire, a hearth fire with wooden logs, something Dowager Stokes enjoyed. In fact, said the colonel, she enjoyed nothing more than stripping naked and lying down by the fire, warming herself up on her deep pile rug. Funnily enough, this bit of knowledge caused Ruff to find another gear and, if it was possible, make the car go even faster, soon they were doing nearly 150 miles an hour. Pretty soon they arrived at the dowager's house, but what was behind those doors? thought Ruff. Was she concealing the information that they so desperately needed and if so, how do you force a dowager to reveal the information that she has? We'll leave that one to Lady Pottersby, thought Ruff. The car finally arrived at the dowager's gates as Ruff cranked down the window to talk into the box.

"Can I help you?" enquired a voice.

"Here to see the dowager, love," said Ruff in his most coarse voice. It was at this point the colonel cringed as he knew full well what was coming next.

"I'm afraid she is busy, sir," came back the voice. The box went silent aside from a few dull crackles just to assure the listener that the box was still working and anything and everything they said could be heard and yes repeated if need be.

"Colonel Barrington here to speak to the dowager, my good man," said the colonel in his more refined voice. Again, the silence was deafening until a creaking sound as the gates parted. Ruff released the handbrake and they were heading in. To the surprise of Ruff, the dowager's home looked a lot like Buckingham Palace, which as Ruff was informed later, was the idea; the dowager had great respect for the queen and felt that to honour her, the house where she lived should be similar, not the same, just similar. Ruff had never travelled to Buckingham Palace, and he had no idea what it looked like, what he did know, however, was that this was one impressive place.

Ruff kept driving the car in a straight line, hoping to either come to some grass where perhaps he might be able to park the car or to an entrance so that he did not have far to walk as he was not the most agile of people. *It is unlikely*, thought Ruff, *but I think we have travelled at least a mile*. Suddenly, he looked up and saw that they were indeed now in an inner courtyard and unless he did slow down, whatever hid behind the glass door in front of them was going to be introduced the hard way to Ruff/Lady Pottersby's car. Fortunately, Ruff spotted the door and managed to slow down in time. A large black cat sat ensconced in the doorway with its huge tail hanging down swinging like a pendulum as much as to say left or right, if this thing hits you that is it. Ruff had lived in Moontown all his life and was well aware of rules regarding animals and especially cats, some things he thought did not bear thinking about. Ruff pulled his huge frame out of the small green car, soon to be followed by the colonel who managed to make a more dignified exit as the two men headed toward the opening and the door. Once they reached it another box awaited them, obviously someone was very security conscious thought Ruff. One of many things that Ruff learned was, do not make the same mistake twice, his failure to make it past the first box proved that it would be unlikely to work a second time, so for this one Ruff stepped aside and allowed the more experienced man to do the meet and greet. Ruff was a perfect gentleman, but everyone has mannerisms and calling everyone love was his, as the colonel called most people blighters, but this particular blighter was like Lady Pottersby and not overly desirous of strangers. The buzz came through again as the colonel pressed it down hard. "Courtyard," said a simple voice.

"Colonel Barrington," he said simply, causing the door to open and a small camera to start revolving on its axis. They were now inside the dowager's inner sanctum, the question was, what happened now?

"Wonder if she needs any work doing?" said Ruff helping himself to a good scratch as bits of dead skin flew off his fingers.

"Today, you are Detective Ruff. When this is finally over, if we are both still here, then you go back to being builder worker Ruff, you understand?" asked the colonel. Without warning, a smell of flowers hit their noses, not unpleasant, just unusual, when you visit someone, you do not expect to be drowned in the smell of flowers especially when you cannot see them. Finally, after going up down and all around the corridors, they finally came upon a small brown wooden door. Could she be behind here? The brown door opened to a pantry, considerably smaller than the one at home but a pantry, nonetheless.

"Fancy a sandwich, love?" Ruff shouted to the colonel.

"No, but I'll have some caviar if there are some biscuits to put them on."

Ruff circled the pantry, opening the doors and cupboards in sequence until he found a small blue pot containing what looked like semolina pudding except it was black. "Is this it?" he remarked, this caused the colonel to take a closer examination of the find. The colonel peeled back the lid and took a good deep breath, and he discovered that it was indeed caviar. Now the hunt was on to find some crackers because as everyone knew, thought Ruff, where there is caviar, logic dictates that there must be crackers. The two men eventually found what they were looking for and grabbed themselves a stool each in the pantry, placing themselves at a table and starting to eat.

"What have you, old boy?" enquired the colonel.

"Some men like caviar," said Ruff, "others like obscenely large sandwiches," as he tried to cram two large doorstops into his mouth. Almost in the same breath, small footsteps could be heard heading to the area, Ruff was the first to hear them as he secreted himself behind where the door would be when it was open, bottle in hand.

"Stop it" said the Colonel. He pointed out that if it was an animal, he would indeed kill it by smashing a bottle over his head and then he was facing a death sentence for cruelty to animals. So, after chatting it over, the two men decided to stand side by side and show no fear as whoever was coming in was no match for two grown boys. Soon their mettle would be tested as Ruff looked ahead and saw the gold door handle starting to twist and give the familiar click sound. As the door slowly came open, lo and behold, a woman, rather tallish, came in. *Is this the dowager?* thought Ruff. The lady looked quite tall with mousy brown hair, but face-wise she looked as though she could pass for a schoolgirl. From a distance, she looked about 14. *Is this a very good facelift?* thought Ruff.

"Hello," screeched the voice, causing Ruff to cover his ears.

"Hello, love, I'm Ruff and this is me mate, the colonel. We have come to ask some questions about Shaun Mayors."

Something was very wrong thought Ruff as she looked as though she was about to vomit. All of a sudden, her gaze was fixed on the colonel as though she either did not understand the last sentence or she was quite literally begging the colonel to translate the last announcement into English.

The stunned, bewildered expression that had found its home in her features was still there, and it appeared as though the colonel would have to say or do something. "My dear, we need some information about these murders, you were at the party, weren't you?" enquired the colonel.

Finally, the look fled from her face and her normal one returned. "Who is your friend?" she announced.

"This is Ruff, he is an eccentric millionaire," announced the colonel. A short moment ensued when everyone kind of had a massive stare-off, no one said anything. Still, the most important thing was, did she really believe what the colonel had said a few minutes ago.

"How many houses do you possess, my good man?" asked the dowager.

Ruff looked both confused and bewildered at the same time. He was now acting like someone who had jumped into a swimming pool to save someone who was drowning and then suddenly realised he was desperately out of his depth. Ruff did not have a clue what to say. "I, the thing is, love," stumbled Ruff, it was almost too painful for the colonel to watch. Lord only knows, he did not really like the big bruiser, but they had gotten a lot closer. Just then an idea flashed on inside the colonel's mind, he knew it was a long shot but what were long shots for if not to try out.

"He's kind of a friend of the family, he is a retired millionaire, but before he became one, he was a handyman, and I hired him to help me out, me dear. You know what I'm like when it comes to jobs around the old house."

Silence stole the air. Would it work or wouldn't it? The colonel was on a knife-edge of despair and desperation, the dowager may hold all or at least most of the answers, and if she did not buy his story, the colonel could see the door behind him getting bigger and bigger ready to suck him through like an emergency door being opened when a plane is in flight. Finally, she spoke. "Oh, I know what you mean, I am terrible, my husband is worse if it can be that way. Tell me, my man, are you free at all to help me?" she asked.

Ruff thought for a moment. "I'd have to check my diary, love, I can let you know," said Ruff in his normal workman type voice.

"Splendid!" she came back. "Now, Barrington, what was it you needed to know?"

There is an old expression on earth, a weight lifted off your shoulders. For the colonel, this was about 10 different weights thrown off his shoulders one at a time, for the first time in a long time, he felt free. Colonel Barrington explained about all the murders and how Lady Pottersby had now lost her butler due to someone shutting him up, professional style, and now they had to figure out the killer's next move before they executed it. Colonel Barrington explained that maybe Shaun Mayors was behind it or knew someone who was behind it and what indeed, if anything, could she say about the party? Could she, in fact, shed any new light on an investigation which was growing stranger and stranger by the minute.

Words poured out of the colonel's mouth as she hoovered them all up like a vacuum but, thought Ruff, once she was full, would she pay out like a penny falls machine or would she simply take the information and lead them down completely the wrong path? Ruff looked at the dowager and then back at the colonel to see if he could tell by the expression on his face what would happen next. Then it happened, the dowager began to speak. The dowager said that Shaun Mayors was indeed a drug dealer but not one of the big boys, he was, in fact, one in what they would call a chain. The Mr Big was someone she did not know, but what she did know is that the Mr Big, whoever it was, did have it in for Lady Pottersby. She also revealed what she believed to be the cause of the murders;

somewhere in the grounds of Pottersby Mansion was a drug plant, and when she said a drug plant she meant a drug plant, literally thousands of marijuana plants and also a facility to process cocaine. In fact, hidden in this one room, they had the ability to make anything they fancied. When asked about the cathinones, she said she had heard them talk about it at the party and the one man who could indeed reveal the name of Mr Big was Harry Queets.

As soon as Ruff heard the name, the colour drained from his face. Harry Queets was lying on a slab in the mortuary, and any information he had was with him in heaven. If he knew anything, no one short of a professional psychic was going to get that information from him. The colonel and the dowager continued talking for hours until, eventually, he had all he could extract from her and now he felt it was indeed time they both left. The two men headed back to the car and got inside. "So, what now?" asked Ruff.

"Since we started this, old boy, whenever we had anything to tell each other we convened in the kitchen," said the colonel.

"Yes, so?" said Ruff. His eyes glanced at the colonel staring at him, he knew deep down, the colonel had said all he needed to. It was time to go back to the kitchen for the biggest meeting of their lives since they met. This time, Lady Pottersby must be involved because, for the first time, they were almost certain her life was now in mortal danger from the killer.

In that car, getting from the dowager's house to Lady Pottersby's mansion did not take long, which was just as well as they had so much to say and they were not sure exactly how much time they now had to tell it. They had a killer and a motive and a possible target, unfortunately for everyone concerned, no one knew who the killer actually was. The two men reconvened in the kitchen, this time bringing Lady Pottersby down the stairs.

"You say you have the killer," she said excitedly, "well, who is it?"

The old lady's face dropped when they explained that while they had the killer and indeed a possible motive, they did not know who in actual fact it was. The biggest clue lay with someone who was already dead. Was this convenient or was this like Jarvis, a person in the wrong place at the wrong time who needed to be shut up and had now for whatever reason had been shut up permanently? The old lady's face dropped even more as they finally broke this news to her, "Cheer up, love," said Ruff, "I'll protect you." At this, Lady Pottersby looked very pleased, and Ruff could swear he saw a smile appear across her face. "At least I will try my best," he added, which did not inspire confidence.

The two men helped put the old lady to bed. When they arrived back at the kitchen, Ruff filled the kettle and started to boil it as he took two cups off the cup hanger just above him. "So now what?" he asked the colonel talking over his shoulder.

"I am afraid we wait, old boy, there is nothing else we can do," said the colonel. At this point, Ruff returned to the table with two steaming cups of coffee. As he handed over the coffee to the colonel, Ruff sat his huge buttocks down on the bench so as his trademark became visible. Fortunately for him, this was not one for the colonel to witness as he was turned the other way.

"We have another option open to us, love," said Ruff.

The colonel looked intrigued. "What is that, old boy?" he asked.

"We don't know the killer, but we can be pretty sure of a motive. Agreed?" said Ruff. The colonel nodded in agreement as he took a sip of his coffee. "We force them out into the open," said Ruff.

"Force them out sounds like a good plan, old boy, but how are you going to do it?" asked the colonel.

Ruff pondered for a minute as he started to drink his coffee. He realised there was no realistic way that they could use the only lady as bait as, due to her age, she was probably less agile than Ruff if such a thing were possible. And if she died, then although he would miss her, himself and the colonel would become the next target as, thought Ruff, it is more than likely this person is killing to protect his investment, which is lurking somewhere in this building. Thinking to himself, Ruff decided on a possible solution.

"Gone to sleep, old boy?" said the colonel.

"No, I have the answer. We obviously cannot use the old lady as bait, and I think you would agree that the only motive we have that seems to make a lick of sense is that the killer is protecting his drug area as I would imagine it is his only source of income. Now, as we cannot unmask the killer as neither of us knows who it is, and our main source of help is unfortunately dead, we need to cut off their supply route. We do that and they will have to come after us then we will have them, at least their identity anyway."

The colonel looked at Ruff with an expression that was a cross between, I have no idea what you just said, and I agree but isn't it a bit risky? Once again, silence enveloped the air until the colonel made his opinion heard. "Splendid idea, old boy, you see I said there was a detective in you somewhere."

"Somewhere," muttered Ruff under his breath.

Just as Ruff finished his coffee, the colonel spoke, "I am sorry, old boy, I think I have spotted a flaw. Neither of us knows where the drug den is, we know it's in the grounds, but Lady Pottersby's mansion is not exactly small is it? And we have assumed that Lady Pottersby is the next victim, so forgive me if I am wrong but time is not exactly our friend is it?"

"We just have to find it, we know it is here, it cannot be that hard. Anyway, the chances are when he or she realises what we are doing they will come after us anyway. I mean look what happened to Jarvis," said Ruff.

The colonel still had some of his coffee left as he was not such a fast drinker as Ruff. He took a drink then thought and drank and thought, eventually, it came to him. "There is one man who may know the answers we need, Harry Queets." Ruff looked at the colonel.

"Harry is dead," said Ruff simply.

"Harry is dead, correct, but he can still talk," said the colonel.

"I am not doing a séance," said Ruff, "you will be giving me nightmares. I think I've already lost a couple of stone after worrying about being caught grave robbing, knowing full well what could happen to me if we were caught, which, incidentally, we could have been," said Ruff.

"Have you ever seen those programmes on the telly where some bounder comes on and says I speak for the dead?" said the colonel.

Ruff thought for a moment, trying to recall programmes he had watched on television. A fat lot he had watched, he thought, he should have been home with his feet up and a bag of crisps and some beer watching the game working on his heart attack. Then it struck him, *yes, I do remember, I don't remember the name, but I remember the programme.* "Yes," announced Ruff, then he paused, "you don't mean?"

The colonel decided it was his turn to have some fun as Ruff thought his name was so funny. "Yes, we are going back to the mortuary in the morning to see Harry and Ralph," said the colonel as he rose to retire to his bedroom as he wanted to sleep for whatever was left of the night.

As the colonel left, Ruff could not resist a parting shot, "Have you never noticed anything odd about that mortician, I think he enjoys his work too much, he has probably eloped with Harry." It was at this point that Ruff knew that he was, in fact, talking to himself and the colonel had long since left the room and vanished.

Ruff got up and started to clean the pots as all of a sudden, a violent thunderstorm came crashing down outside the window, causing Ruff to jump just for a second. As he turned, Jarvis was standing behind him. "Can I help you, sir?" his voice boomed out as from behind his back a huge axe appeared and came crashing down on Ruff slicing his body in two, killing him instantly.

Ruff awoke with someone slapping his face. As his eyes began to focus, he could see it was the lady. "Oh, thank heavens, Ruff, I thought I had lost you. Barrington, there is no need for an ambulance." Ruff struggled to his feet as Lady Pottersby made a concerted effort to help him to a chair.

"What happened?" asked Ruff.

"No idea, my good man. Barrington came down as he does every morning for his breakfast and to bring me something, as he does, now we have lost Jarvis." Ruff stopped her there.

"Jarvis, he was here," said Ruff.

"What, here in the kitchen, but that is impossible, he is dead," said Lady Pottersby.

"What's impossible?" asked the colonel.

"Ruff here saw Jarvis last night," said Lady Pottersby.

"How? He is dead," said the colonel.

"He was here in the kitchen. I was washing the cups, I turned, and he said, can I help you, sir? Then he sliced me in two with an axe," said Ruff looking at Lady Pottersby and the colonel.

"Did you wash the cups last night?" asked the colonel.

"No, they are there on the floor where I fell," said Ruff.

The colonel walked over to the cups and got two pencils out of the drawers. Lifting the two cups by their handles, he placed them on the unit before getting two plastic bags from the drawers. "What are you doing?" asked Ruff.

The colonel sat down next to him and looked Ruff straight in the eyes. "Last night after talking to you, I went straight to sleep, I never go straight to sleep, I need tablets to make me sleep. Then you see a dead man kill you. Our drinks were laced with drugs. Whoever the killer is, knows what we are up to, and this I am afraid was just a warning; next time, old boy, I do not think either of us will be here. I think we need to unmask this killer as soon as possible and get back to our normal lives before we have no lives to go back to," said the colonel.

The colonel's car was a classic, cream-coloured one with no roof and a tyre on the back, the seats were red leather, and it seated four. It was very uncomfortable for long journeys as the leather had nothing to it and you would find your back pressed against hard leather. The car was also quite slow, but on the plus side, it was a classic car, and you try getting to colonel to sell it, to say you would struggle would be an understatement. Finally, the two men pulled up at the mortuary ready to see Ralph, hopefully for the last time – hopefully in that they hoped there would be no more dead bodies for him to examine. As far as the colonel was concerned, he wanted Harry Queets to be the last body and to hold all the answers to their problems, and also to find out who was chasing the three of them before it was too late. The two men entered the mortuary and were greeted by a worried-looking Ralph in the reception. "Hello, gentlemen, and what can I do for you?" asked Ralph.

The colonel handed the two cups to Ralph and explained what had happened last night. Immediately, Ralph took the cups to be analysed, saying that tomorrow he would have some answers as to what was in the cups if indeed there was anything there. When Ruff mentioned about Jarvis, Ralph did not look surprised, in fact he looked as though he understood what had happened. "Dark shadow," said Ralph. The two men looked at each other, dark shadow they thought, and once again they looked at Ralph. Ralph explained that last night he was working late in the mortuary when he popped out for a cup of coffee. When he came back in, the fridge containing Harry had been opened, and his body was no longer there, someone had stolen it. He looked all over the mortuary and then decided after about an hour to give in and phone the police to report a break-in. As he came back toward the fridges to look one last time before calling the police, a dark shadow appeared on the wall and stayed there. Ralph ran out and tried to get some fresh air and compose himself. After a while, he re-entered the mortuary, and there was no shadow on the wall, and Harry was sealed back in his fridge.

Part Eight

Ruff the Detective

At this point, Ruff looked as though perhaps the mists were starting to clear in his head. After a while, the colonel caught his glance. "What is it, old boy?" asked the colonel.

Ruff did not answer but instead continued to look at the body. "I think I know," said Ruff.

The colonel looked at him. "You know who did this?" said the colonel.

Again, Ruff started to ponder and look very deep in thought which was unusual for him. "I think so, and why, but before I tell you, I need to check some things out," said Ruff. Ruff walked over to the body of Harry. "What can you tell us about him?" asked Ruff, there was a long silence as the mortician walked off to get his papers.

After a short while, Ralph came back with a stack of papers and clutching his head. "Sorry, bit of a migraine," said Ralph. "Well, what can I say, Harry appears to have had a heart attack," said Ralph.

"Natural?" asked Ruff.

"No, it looks like it was induced by some kind of drug or trauma, it's hard to tell which, even if I had more time, however his arteries were very furred," said the mortician.

"So, you're saying he was on the reserve list even if he had not died?" said Ruff.

The mortician looked at him. "It's not a polite way of putting it, but yes he was on borrowed time," said Ralph.

"Was this marijuana or cocaine?" asked Ruff.

"He was on cocaine in that we found it in his urine, but he was on painkillers, so this could account for it; however, there was marijuana in his body," said Ralph.

Ruff looked deeper in thought, the more information he found out. "So, it is possible that the marijuana brought on the heart attack?" said Ruff.

Ralph pondered for a moment before answering. "It is possible, marijuana is a very dangerous drug which can cause hallucinations and paranoia. Considering the state of his arteries, I would imagine that it would not take a great deal to have pushed him over the edge," said Ralph.

Ruff did not speak for a moment as he thought of what to say next. "So, it is possible that someone gave the marijuana to him rather than him voluntarily taking it himself?" said Ruff.

"Marijuana can be taken in many different ways, so someone may have put it into him rather than him taking it by choice. But the cocaine, he had many illnesses so the cocaine may have been from the painkillers, it is hard to tell as the amount in his system was not high," said Ralph.

"I thought marijuana was safe to use; indeed, some people use it for medicinal purposes," said the colonel. Ralph looked at him.

"It's like most things, in moderation, there may not be a problem, but each person is different. Sometimes in medicine, we use something called marijuana tinctures, these are liquids extracted from marijuana plants that are infused with a solution of alcohol or alcohol and water. The person places a few drops under the tongue. This is highly concentrated, highly potent and fast-acting, it produces a very intense high. If he did this or someone did it to him, with his heart, I doubt he would live to tell about it," said Ralph.

"So, by George, we have the killer; he raped Lucy and then he went for a joint, had a bad vision, scared him to death because of his heart and he died, case closed," said the colonel.

Ruff looked at him with a disapproving glance. "Have you ever known anything that simple, love? No, I don't think he did it. I think the killer gave him one of these tinctures and his heart gave out," said Ruff.

The colonel did not like to be challenged. "Impossible, old boy, what about the semen in Lucy?"

Ralph spoke. "She was raped, there was evidence of damage indicating a struggle and, yes, the semen belonged to Harry, but he didn't put it up her, someone else did," said Ralph. The colonel looked even more confused than he did about five minutes ago. "The sample was lifted from the laboratory, and it was inserted manually. Queets was a gynaecologist; if anyone could do it, he could," said Ralph.

"So now, who is the killer, Ruff?" asked the colonel.

"I guess I know, but I cannot ask Lady Pottersby to get me an arrest warrant, all I have is my theory, it is a strong theory but a theory nonetheless," said Ruff.

The next stop for the men was to head back to the mansion. Saying their goodbyes, they left Ralph for what they hoped would be the last time. As the two men headed back down the road, the colonel turned to Ruff and asked the obvious question, "So, old boy, who did this?"

Ruff looked at him half concentrating on the road and half on the colonel. "I guess you know it is wrong to call someone a liar if you have no proof, it is also unwise to call someone a killer if you cannot prove it. I have been thinking and thinking, and I have a clear picture as to our killer, but we need to catch him first. You see, I think this whole thing was drug-related, the rose hips, the little creatures on the plants, they all tied in so nice. Our killer was trying to use Lady Pottersby to further his drug business but, like any good business, it can only be successful if people allow it to be so. The problem the killer had was this, Lady Pottersby was ideal, she is an elderly rich lady with many, many high up connections going as far as the royal family. Now, if someone suspected drug dealings in her house, no one would dare come out and say it because of who she is," said Ruff.

"I see, so what you're saying is, because of who she is, the killer gave himself carte blanche to do what he needed to," said the colonel.

"Precisely," said Ruff, "the only problem was that while Lady Pottersby was above suspicion, you can hardly deny what you see with your own two eyes. I mean, love, it is one thing to come out and say, I think I saw drug activity at the mansion, it is quite another when you saw it with your own two eyes," said Ruff.

The colonel looked in awe and admiration at Ruff. "Looks like that murder mystery weekend paid off," said the colonel, "So these people all died because of what they saw?"

Ruff turned and looked at the colonel. "I hope so, or I am going to look pretty stupid, love."

The car carried on down the road heading back to the mansion, the two men for the first time now confident of catching the killer. But what of Lady Pottersby? thought the colonel. If the killer really is somewhere in her mansion, then it would stand to reason that the next obstacle in the way would be her. "Is Lady Pottersby in danger, old boy?" said the colonel to Ruff.

He pondered for a moment with his brow furrowed, he stopped shortly before answering as if it was a question that did not require an answer. "I do not think so. You see, my theory is, the killer is killing because of what the others have seen, let's run through them," said Ruff.

The colonel relaxed back in his seat as Ruff began to reveal his theory. "The first murder was Evelyn Trubshaw, she had her hand removed and a drug on her lips, but remember, she was strangled, the hand was removed to distract us, the drug was a muscle relaxant to stop her screaming out and drawing attention. You see, very few people enter Lady Pottersby's mansion so she would not put restrictions on who goes where. I suspect the killer had no intention of killing Evelyn but had to because of the possibility that she saw his drugs factory in the house. I mean, I cannot think of any other reason, she works out of a paper shop, I mean you saw her body she was hardly likely to put up a fight," said Ruff. The colonel was digesting what Ruff was saying as though in some bizarre way it was starting to make sense. "You see it just goes to show that you can never underestimate people, love. OK, so the chances are she would not have put up a fight, but she had a good strong voice, what if she screamed out and someone stronger than the killer appeared. We are not just talking about murder; we are also talking about drugs worth lord knows how much street value. So combining everything, the risk was too great, so to be on the safe side, she was drugged to stop her making a noise, her hand was removed to create a distraction, while the real reason for death was strangulation. On to the second body," said Ruff.

The colonel started to think, the second murder was Bertha, and that was nothing short of brutal, but how and why was indeed a mystery. Let's see Ruff get a theory out of that, thought the colonel. "Bertha," said the colonel.

"That is right, Bertha, but why her? It took me ages to figure this one, love. She was brutally murdered and drugged, and to be honest, it took me a while to figure it out. Evelyn was murdered for a reason; the hand was a distraction. I think that Bertha was murdered because of the tape. Bertha was a large lady and well built, she would have put up one hell of a fight. Now compare this to Trubshaw, she is a little girl who works at a paper shop, you could probably kill her without trying, but I reckon Bertha would have fought back and again I am guessing, but I reckon the three meat hooks were kind of to embarrass her."

"Embarrass her?" said the colonel.

"The killer realised that when the body was discovered, people would see her like that, and I think it was partly to embarrass her and partly anger. You see, love, I think it comes down to the tape."

The colonel looked at Ruff with surprise, he had forgotten all about it. "Ah yes, the tape," said the colonel, "did it really exist?"

"I think it did, this is where the third murder comes in, the teacher Puktar. I think he was having an affair with Evelyn or maybe it was even rape. I think an affair was more likely as no sign of rape appeared at the post-mortem. But again, my theory is the killer wanted that tape. When Bertha refused and said she would not give it or did not have it, whatever she said, I guess it made him angry and he lost control, making the death even more brutal. Think about it, if this was his motive, why did he not kill Evelyn in a brutal fashion? Everything he did to her can be accounted for," said Ruff.

"Mr Puktar?"

"If the tape exists, there is something on there that frames either Puktar or the killer as you saw the look on his face when the tape was mentioned, and I was conveniently drugged at the college when I asked about it. No, I think that tape does exist, and we need to find it," said Ruff.

The colonel was listening intently as all the pieces slid into place, but questions still remained. "So why the elaborate charade with Puktar and pretending he had committed suicide?" he said.

"Think about it, the motive. Evelyn was the same, she had her hand cut off to make it look like blood loss when in fact she was strangled; this killer knows what he is doing."

The colonel thought for a moment. But what about Bertha? he thought. "What about Bertha? There was no charade, she died from numerous meat hooks inserted into her."

"In murder, my love, sometimes people don't always follow the same pattern, it confuses police detectives into thinking there is more than one killer when in fact there is just one. Bertha was rage, pure aggression, to prove a point if you will. Evelyn and Puktar were a threat to him so they had to go."

"Tell me about Puktar, why was it meant to look like suicide?" said the colonel. Ruff continued on his way as the car snaked its way to the mansion.

"Puktar was killed by drugs in his system according to the post-mortem, someone, presumably the killer injected drugs into him. Whether the killer was listening and thought it would be believable, him committing suicide, I don't know, but it's my only theory for that one," said Ruff.

"How so, old boy?" said the colonel.

"Puktar was supposed to be having an affair or trying to at least with Evelyn, maybe that is what is on the tape if it exists. So, what better way? Think about it, kinky teacher tries to get it on with one of his pupils, she runs to the police, he hangs himself in desperation. It seems too simple, but it does make perfect sense." said Ruff.

As Ruff spoke more and more, the colonel became impressed to the point that he forgot who he was talking to. Was this really a building worker? he thought or was this really a detective on his holidays? Let's test him some more, thought the colonel. "What about the headless body, old boy?"

Ruff thought for a moment, this was one he had definitely not prepared for. "Her name was Amy Pottersby," said Ruff.

"You mean?" said the colonel.

"Lady Pottersby's sister. When she found out, she was mortified. She found out when the mortician found a strange mark on her arm," said Ruff.

"What was it?" asked the colonel.

"It was the coat of arms of the Pottersby house, the head was removed to stop identification, but like all the others, she was drugged. The killer realised that Lady Pottersby would know straight away who it was, that is why he did it," said Ruff.

"I am forgetting Lucy," announced the colonel.

"Ah, yes, love, the fourth murder. She had her breasts removed, but again, cause of death was drugs, the same drug as the others," said Ruff.

"So why—" said the colonel, Ruff cut him off.

"So why the breasts? Lucy was early twenties and still a virgin, I know this because the post-mortem revealed it. When

I was in the room, she kept exposing her breasts to me, but I am not that kind of man. I knew she did not want me; she was embarrassed that she was still a virgin, she was a good-looking girl, but she was shy," said Ruff.

"Doesn't sound that way, old boy," said the colonel.

"She was, very shy but if she thought someone really wanted her, then she would lose her inhibitions. I guess she thought the killer was going to finally make her a woman, so she whips them out and he—" said Ruff.

"Whips them off," said the colonel.

"Exactly," said Ruff.

The colonel thought, who else had they not talked about? Jarvis. "What about the butler, old boy? He had no drugs in him."

"No, but it was drug-related. Jarvis was about to reveal to me who killed everyone, it was at that time that theories started to swirl round my head. There was a man, Simon Mere, he was one of the people that I interviewed, he said that he heard an argument, it went on for a while, but some of it revolved around the missing tape. People who he could not see talked about Bertha having possession of the tape and he says he thinks that someone was hit. Now assuming that person was the killer, it means that the tape does in fact exist and all the answers are there, but it does not explain why Bertha was killed unless he got the information from her before she died, so we have to assume he did. Then the incident with Jarvis. I asked him if he had hit Walter Bens, but Jarvis said no, the man he hit— And that is when I had bits of Jarvis all over me," said Ruff. The colonel thought for a moment.

"So, we have to assume that whoever Jarvis did hit is indeed the killer."

"Or knows who it is and it trying to cover up for them," said Ruff.

"Shaun Mayors?" asked the colonel.

"Shaun Mayors is an interesting one. I think he was killed as a drug-related death. Those roses stuffed in his mouth, they were rose hips and I think they were connected to why he was killed, but it is the one death we know very little about. I have asked Ralph to look further into it and, hopefully, he should have something in the morning and if it is what I hope, it should be just a case of setting the trap and springing it," said Ruff. The colonel had one last question.

"So, what about Queets and the semen in Lucy?" said the colonel.

"There was indeed semen in Lucy's vagina, but it was placed there not by an act of sex, it was manually inserted by a qualified gynaecologist," said Ruff.

"Queets?" said the colonel.

"Before he died, I would say yes, don't ask me the how and why. You want that, and I guess Ralph will explain, but Queets died of coronary artery disease but with the help of the marijuana tinctures supplied by our friend the killer," said Ruff as he pulled the car up to Pottersby mansions.

"So, Queets was in the way?" said the colonel.

"Shall we say, Queets was dangerous, love. If what comes back about Mayors' death is what I think, it should make my job easier."

"What about the drug factory, does it even exist?" said the colonel.

"I believe so, and I think when we find it, like when you stir up a hornets' nest, everything and I mean everything associated with this murder including the killer will be revealed, along with the tape," said Ruff.

"Tell me you know the location, old boy," said the colonel.

"I am afraid not, we will have to find it, preferably tonight as tomorrow, hopefully, we will get our final post-mortem report."

The conversation continued until the vehicle pulled up at the mansion, and now finally the hunt was on to find this drugs laboratory if indeed it did exist. The two men left the vehicle, but instead of heading back to the kitchen as they usually did, Ruff decided that it would be better if the two men went back to their rooms to think about how they would find this drug lab. Ruff's huge frame went back to his bedroom and collapsed down onto the bed. The huge man lay back on the bed and began to think. How does someone find a drugs lab? Surely Lady Pottersby would be aware of it, the size of the lab must have been huge, can someone really hide something of that size? In the back of his mind, Ruff knew who had done all these murders and was pretty sure he had a motive, but now he had to prove it. Could he possibly bring him out, what about the tape, should he be concentrating on the tape? As these thoughts swirled around his head, a loud rap came on the door. "Can I come in?"

"Yes," said Ruff. The colonel entered the room and began to walk around, taking in every part of it, looking at the bathroom, looking out of the window. As the colonel looked out the window, it was hard to make out anything as it was the night-time, but through the mists of darkness, he could make out a small white light. On closer inspection, it was a man. At this point, the colonel called over Ruff, who did his best to slide off the bed and waddle over to the window. As he looked out, he too saw the white light, this he realised could be the break he needed. Now to spring the trap.

Ruff pulled back from the window and sat on his bed with the colonel, and the two men started to formulate a plan to catch the killer. Ruff left the room with the colonel, and the two men made their way down the corridor looking for anything that might give them a clue as to the whereabouts of the drug lab. Then Ruff remembered something, that night when he was in the corridor alone and something strange happened. Were the two things connected? Desperately, his mind raced, could he piece together those events from all that time ago and did they have anything to do with all these murders? As we go through life, people say things to you which stay with you for a long time, Ruff was starting to remember as though a light had gone on in his head. That was it, he thought, I left Sarah in the kitchen, the lights went out, and all the odd things started to happen, and I woke up face-first on the kitchen floor. Yes, he thought, I do remember.

Quickly, Ruff explained his event to the colonel, to which the colonel replied that he remembered, this was when you had wardrobe bowels. Ruff looked indignant and repeated that he did not have wardrobe bowels, nor was he hallucinating, this was all done by Charles Clearwater. The colonel looked stunned, asking him to repeat the name to which Ruff obliged. "Are you saying, old boy, that Charles is the killer?"

Ruff was more than a little reluctant but nodded his head. "That is my belief, love, but as I said, it is circumstantial, we need to find that lab, and then we'll know if I am right."

The colonel still looked completely stunned. Charles Clearwater was obscenely wealthy, anything he did not own he did not want. He had the money to buy and sell Ruff many times over, he had the money to buy and sell members of the royal family. What on earth would Lady Pottersby make of Ruff when she knew who he was accusing? "I cannot believe it, old boy, accusing him, how can you be sure?" said the colonel still disbelieving everything Ruff had said.

"I had a long chat with him, and everything he says, everywhere he claims to be, ties up with the murders. And remember what you said."

"What, old boy?" said the colonel obviously wanting to be reminded.

"You said he had the money to buy and sell even members of the royal family," said Ruff.

"Yes, so?" said the colonel.

"Even buy his own distractions?" said Ruff.

The colonel took a little time before he replied, and finally, he nodded in defeat. "Yes, I suppose so, but we still have no motive," said the colonel.

"Drugs," replied Ruff.

"Drugs?" said the colonel.

"Think about it," said Ruff. "If you want to start in the drugs business, what is the one thing you need? A backer, a money backer, someone who has so much money he does not know what to do with it, and if anyone gets heavy, he has the money to hire someone to shut them up." The colonel looked intrigued.

"The plan was perfect," said Ruff. "Charles never risked anything, all he had to do was kill people, if he was ever caught, he just bought their silence, love," said Ruff.

The colonel was starting to believe but still needed some more convincing. "OK, old boy, let's go to the kitchen, you have some explaining to do," said the colonel.

The two men entered the kitchen as was becoming a habit for them. The colonel went over and started to make the coffee as Ruff sat down at the table looking more relieved now as finally someone else knew what he had known for ages, and he could explain his theory. The colonel arrived momentarily back at the table with two mugs of coffee freshly poured. The colonel positioned himself opposite Ruff and looked at him, not breaking his gaze. "So, let's start. Evelyn, why?"

"Evelyn was killed because of what she knew, as were most of them. Many people suspected Charles but like me had no proof. Working in a paper shop, she saw many people and heard many things, all it took was for one person to mention the possibility and that would be reason enough. Also, she was friends with Bertha, so she confided what she knew to Bertha, knowing full well no one else would take her serious," said Ruff.

"Why would Bertha?" said the colonel.

"You yourself said no one would talk to her. Besides Bertha, she befriended her, she helped her, it stands to reason if she had something this big to spill, she would have to tell someone," said Ruff.

"Charles," said the colonel.

"You forget, Charles was always here, he was a guest at the party along with the rest of them. It is possible that Charles overheard them talking. Now put yourself in his shoes. You have a multimillion drug plant operating, and there is one young girl who knows too much or who you suspect knows too much, what do you do? Do you risk it and allow her to destroy it all before it has even started? Charles was a strong, fully grown man, it would take no effort to kill her," said Ruff.

"What about the drugs on her lips?" said the colonel.

"What do people do more than anything at parties?" said Ruff.

"Take drugs, by God," said the colonel flexing his moustache. "Ruff, you have me intrigued, onto the next one."

"You must remember though, love, the drugs were put there by Charles, she never took them. The drugs in her system were injected, it says so on the post-mortem," said Ruff. "Bertha was murder number two but the easiest one to fathom, she was killed because of what she knew or what Charles thought she knew."

"How so, old boy?" said the colonel.

"The tape exists. I have not heard it, but when I do, I would bet you anything it will have a conversation on it regarding the drugs deal with Charles. You see, Evelyn recorded the conversation with Puktar because Puktar wanted to have sex with her, so she needed some kind of evidence. But Puktar was so friendly to her, part of her gave in, and she started telling him about Charles and the drugs. Bertha found out about the tape as Evelyn told her because they were friends. The fight that happened, that Mayors heard, was Charles and Bertha arguing. Charles wanted the location of the tape, and he knew that Bertha could tell him where it was hidden," said Ruff.

"She refused?" said the colonel.

"Correct. Bertha was a fully grown adult, not some weak paper shop girl. When Bertha was killed, it was not so much anger, it was all he could do, he literally had to kill her the way he did. Bertha was heavily into sexual equality; she could not allow a man to beat her in a fight or to appear stronger than her. So, to embarrass her when she was dead, Charles mutilated the body but again, she was too strong, so he gave her drugs to make her weaker again intravenously."

"Puktar you mentioned, but why did he die, surely he would have revealed where the tape was?" said the colonel.

"Given time he might have, but Charles had it in his mind that Puktar knew where the tape was and he was hiding it," said Ruff.

"For what reason?" asked the colonel.

"That is a simple answer. Charles believed that he was hiding the tape and he would simply wipe the information about his come-on with Evelyn and take the rest to the police so he could claim a reward. So when he told Charles he did not know the location of the tape, he was telling the truth, but—" said Ruff.

"Charles did not believe him," said the colonel. The colonel's eyes were wide with admiration. This man was a builder who had been on a murder mystery weekend, and he was on the brink of solving a crime most detectives would have struggled to solve. And also, with his unfortunate ability to choose trousers that did not fit his over ample cleavage, bring some amusement to the proceedings.

"You OK, love?" asked Ruff.

"Yes, I'm fine, old boy, onto the next one," said the colonel.

"Lucy was what you would lovingly call an airhead. She took nothing serious. She had one mission in life, to feel a man, any man inside her. It's kind of sad, love," said Ruff with a sadness in his eyes.

"How do you know that, old boy?" said the colonel.

"She tried it on with me. If you want to sleep with me, you must be desperate," said Ruff laughing. "So, she tried it on with Charles, he kept spurning her advances."

"So?" said the colonel.

"She was a chambermaid, she heard things," said Ruff.

"She heard?" said the colonel.

"She heard about the drugs, but Charles did not know. Lucy made sexual advances toward him, and when he refused, she threatened to go to the police with her information unless he fu—" said Ruff.

"Slept with her?" said the colonel.

"Aye, love, that's what I meant to say. Lucy had this idea that men wanted her body so much, so she flashed her chests at men as though this was the prize men had to have. She prized her chests above everything else, so, of course, Charles killed her and sliced them off," said Ruff.

"The headless body?" said the colonel.

"The headless body was a tough one. The body belonged to Amy Pottersby, the sister to Lady Pottersby. Charles knew that when she died, and the body was discovered, Lady Pottersby would know who it was, so he cut off her head, making identification very hard. Unfortunately, the body lay undiscovered for some time and one day it began to smell. Charles noticed this and covered her body with roses, which were unfortunately infected with thrips, which are similar to maggots. And while the smell of the roses was pleasant, the thrips did their work. The thrips were an accident," said Ruff.

"Incidentally, old boy, while you were away, I did some research of my own, and I got a sample of the thrips and found out what they were," said the colonel. Ruff looked intrigued.

"What were they?" asked Ruff.

"They were called frankliniella occidentalis, they are yellowish-white flying bugs," said the colonel. Ruff looked at him.

"That's good, love, but I don't see how it helps?" said Ruff.

"Apparently, they lay their eggs on cannabis plant leaves and destroy them, so if that blighter has these, he will have some serious trouble with his next batch of plants," said the colonel. The two men looked at each other and laughed.

"Oh, yes. Jarvis. I never knew why that blighter was killed; can you explain that?" said the colonel.

Ruff thought for a moment before speaking. "Jarvis was telling me about an argument he had and how he hit someone. He was talking about Walter Bens and how he had developed a synthetic cannabis plant which was similar to cannabis, but the ingredients were not illegal. So, technically if you were caught with it, you could say it was not cannabis and escape the death sentence. The problem is Puktar was given a sample and it caused him hallucinations, shakes, paranoia the whole lot. So I said *you hit Bens* and he said *no I hit*— then someone shot him," said Ruff.

"So why kill him, old boy?" said the colonel.

"Anyone who was given this information would double-check to be sure, considering cannabis carries the death penalty. So once everyone knew it was Charles, he would be investigated and before long, it would all be revealed. And even if it wasn't, do you not think that people would soon start to search for the source of the cannabis manufacturing?" said Ruff.

"Harry Queets," said the colonel.

"Marijuana tinctures under the tongue is how he died, it would not have taken much and, as the mortician said, his arteries were furred, so that was that. Harry was a gynaecologist, no one raped Lucy, but Harry knew what Charles was up to and there is an old saying, there is no honour among thieves, and I guess that goes for criminals as well. So Harry decided that coming out and openly naming Charles as the killer without any proof would be suicide as his claim would have to be investigated, and in the meantime, Charles had ample time to kill him remembering he was only a suspect and not a definite murderer. Unfortunately for Harry, someone got wind of this and when he placed the semen inside Lucy, that someone told Charles, leading him to administer the tinctures and kill him," said Ruff.

"Last one. Shaun Mayors," said the colonel.

"Shaun Mayors was a doctor. I found this out talking to Lady Pottersby. But he also had a criminal record for doing things which, to put it politely, would have been considered medically unethical. So, he joined with Charles to share in the drug profits, while Charles was Mr Big, Shaun helped. He would not get directly involved in case it was traced back to him, he provided the tinctures and gave them to Harry. As Shaun was a doctor, why would Harry doubt him? Then when Harry died, Shaun and Charles were free to do what they wanted, Charles with his money and Shaun with his medical knowledge. Unfortunately, Shaun got cold feet and decided that as a doctor, what he was doing was wrong. I do not know if there is a correct time and place to get cold feet, but I suspect this was not it. When Charles realised, he placed the infected roses on Shaun's body after he had murdered him," said Ruff.

"So, Shaun was behind the thrips?" said the colonel.

"Yes, remember, what is one of the subjects studied at medical school?" said Ruff. The colonel thought for a moment.

"Botany, by God!" said the colonel.

"Exactly, love," said Ruff. "Shaun had the knowledge to put the thrips in the plant, that strain of thrips could have destroyed the cannabis plants, and it potentially could have destroyed the entire crop."

"So, when Charles realised what Shaun was up to, he had no choice," said the colonel. He now knew as much as Ruff did and he had the task now of trying to find the drugs lab, the question was, where to start?

The colonel rose to his feet. "Come on then, sir, we must find that blighter's lab and close him down before he commits any more murders."

Ruff did not get to his feet quite as fast as the colonel as though perhaps he was slightly more reluctant than his elderly counterpart. "The thing is, love," started Ruff. The colonel could see a worried look in Ruff's eyes and decided it would probably be a better idea to sit down and hear this one out. "My theory, for what it's worth, is that these people were killed because they provided a threat to Charles's drug business. In other words, if they had not provided a threat, they would never have been killed."

"Where are you going with this, old boy?" said the colonel.

"In order for us to prove my theory, we have to become a threat to Charles. Which means—" said Ruff.

"Which means we become the targets," said the colonel reluctantly.

"I am afraid so, love," said Ruff. "If you want to back out..."

The colonel looked at Ruff then at the floor and then out of the window before finally turning back to Ruff. "Well, I guess I would like some credit in this escapade, so let's do it."

A smile suddenly spread across Ruff's face. "Thank you, Colonel," said Ruff.

"Colonel Buttocks, old boy," said the colonel. The two men headed out the kitchen and into the darkness of the hall. "So where now?" said the colonel.

Ruff looked at him deep in thought. "I guess the best option would be to find the tape first; this will drag him out into the open, then maybe we can force him to reveal where his lab is?" said Ruff.

"Any idea where the tape is?" said the colonel.

Ruff thought for a moment before he spoke. "I have a feeling that the tape is in the college," said Ruff.

"Any reason why, old boy?" said the colonel.

"Bertha was giving a lecture on the morning of her death. I get the feeling she had been given the tape by Evelyn, and she had left the tape somewhere in the college." The colonel thought for a moment.

"Puktar's room," said the colonel.

"The death, I think, was partly in anger. I think Charles knew all along that the tape was there, it was just a question of finding it. The only trouble was, he could not find it. Puktar would never have told him the location even if he knew where it was."

"You know the location of the tape, old boy?" said the colonel.

"To be honest, look at the deaths, as we are talking who knows who is listening, so the answer to your question is maybe, maybe not, love," said Ruff.

The two men headed out back to the car. It was still late at night. Ruff thought, *there won't be anyone around this time at night, leastways, I can't see anyone following us.* But as he walked toward the car, Ruff could not help thinking someone was lurking in the bushes. Ruff got in and started the engine as the car headed to the college to hopefully find the missing tape. After a while, the car pulled up at the college; as one would expect, the college was closed and locked. The colonel got out and walked toward the doors.

"It will be locked, love," said Ruff pulling up his jeans to cover his ample backside.

The colonel pulled out a small case about the size of a glasses case, opening it he pulled out two thin pieces of metal. "Locks are made to be broken into," said the colonel as he inserted the metal and the lock clicked back. The door swung open only for Ruff to almost walk into the back of the colonel as he stopped dead.

"What are you doing, love?" asked Ruff.

"Pressure pads, I'm just trying to figure where they are," said the colonel.

"Pressure pads?" said Ruff. The colonel looked at him.

"Pressure pads are actually cheap, and usually they are silent and connected to the local police station, then we have to explain to them what we are doing breaking into the college," said the colonel.

"How do you know where they are, love?" said Ruff.

"I used to be quite a celebrity because of my heroics in the war. They once got me as a guest speaker and as a reward, rather than giving me money, they gave me a guided tour of the college, showing me the plans and how the new college compared to the old. Got a bit of a photographic memory, old boy, it's just a question of accessing the photos in my mind," said the colonel. Ruff said no more and simply waited for the colonel to make his next announcement, all of a sudden, the colonel piped up. "Yes, I remember now, old boy. It was a zigzag pattern, start on the left, and then you move in a zigzag formation," said the colonel. The two men started zigzagging, which was quite a sight to see, a relatively old man and an overweight building worker. Eventually, just like a game of hopscotch, they made it to the door.

"So where now?" asked Ruff.

The colonel looked at the corridor stretched out in front of them like a giant tongue pointing the way. "Which room?" asked the colonel. Ruff thought for a moment.

"I don't like to say it, but until we get some kind of clue to follow, we will have to use our instincts," said Ruff. Back it went to the colonel as once again he started to think very hard. "Tapes are temperamental, they do not like extreme cold or heat, so the odds are this tape is somewhere not too hot or cold," said Ruff.

"Kitchen's out, old boy, and so's the basement, that's where the boiler is," said the colonel. Ruff tried to think of a response.

"I think the gym will be off-limits as that is very cold, the garages as well."

"What about the library, you could hide it in the books?" The colonel thought it was a good idea, but he could foresee a problem.

"If it was hidden in the books, you have a lot to search." Now it was Ruff's turn.

"I guess the chemistry lab would be unlikely due to the number of chemicals there, one slight accident and then bye-bye tape." Ruff stopped for a moment and then turned around. "So, what would you suggest?" The colonel thoughtfully stroked his chin.

"I don't like saying it but I think that the library is the most likely as it would be the hardest to find, but I also think the English room as it is on the top floor near the safe." Ruff thought about it for a moment.

"What makes you think the English room?" said Ruff.

"Apart from what I have already told you, the English room is neither too hot nor too cold," said the colonel.

"Right, you go to the English room, and I will explore the library," said Ruff.

The two men climbed the stairs before heading off in different directions. Inside the library, the first thing that struck Ruff was the huge numbers of books on the shelves, there must have been thousands. *There must be some way to narrow down the search*, thought Ruff, *what I need is a clue that might tell me something. A clue, subject matter, what did Charles like, could it be that simple? But then again*, thought Ruff, *it if was that simple, I guess Charles would have found it by now.* Ruff began to look through the thousands of books and started to realise he desperately needed help. Just then, the door opened, and Ruff looked up to see his friend stood in the doorway.

"Any luck, old boy?" asked the colonel.

"Too many books I am afraid," said Ruff. "If we only knew his hobbies or interests. I guess it won't be that easy, but at least it's a chance."

As Ruff sat down his enormous behind as he started to rest, the colonel made an announcement, "He liked hunting, old boy, he was a bit of a sportsman."

Ruff looked at him and then down at the floor then back up again at the colonel. "At the risk of offending you, it's not really a sport. Sport is where there is an element of risk involved, the only risk in hunting is if you fall off your horse."

The colonel went beet red and looked as though he would explode. "How can you say that, sir? I do realise if you got on a horse, we would be arrested for cruelty."

Ruff looked at him realising he had offended him. "Sorry, love, no offence meant, it was just my opinion, like boxing, I can't understand boxing being regarded as a sport," said Ruff.

Again, the colonel looked at him in a strange way. "How do you mean, old boy?" said the colonel.

"Well, look at boxing, the object of it is to beat someone so badly that they black out. How is that a sport?"

The colonel carried on looking at him. "I agree with you, old boy, but boxing as you know is banned in Moontown.

Remember, some years ago, the greatest medical brains got together and conclusively proved the damaging blows needed in order to cause someone to pass out is never good. The brain has to hit the head so violently that one person blacks out and frequently the dura mater is damaged beyond repair, causing a hole in the jelly and haemorrhage in the brain."

The colonel started to look through some more books as did Ruff. Then Ruff spoke, "Does her ladyship ever hunt? I know she is a woman but considering her status."

"Her ladyship is against all types of blood sports. By God, she helped to get boxing banned, she helped to bring in the death sentence for killing animals, and she has tried to get hunting banned," said the colonel.

Ruff kept flicking through the books desperately searching for the elusive book. "How are people executed in Moontown?" said Ruff. "I mean, I have heard of it, but I have never seen it."

The colonel put down the book he had found. "The death sentence was something developed over years by the finest legal minds and then ratified by the government. They decided that not only should the death sentence be handed out for the worst of the crimes, they also decided that the death sentence should be very painful. The person should be made to suffer as it was a punishment," said the colonel.

Ruff looked at him. "So, how does it happen?" asked Ruff. The colonel looked at him.

"The person is strapped down to a chair with solid leather bindings, and then a slow-acting poison is introduced into the vein. It starts off as nothing, then as it gradually takes over the body, the pain becomes excruciating to the point where the person is going to pass out, this is all monitored by doctors. When you reach critical incidence and the prisoner is about to pass out, two thick iron ingots are fired by a machine straight into the eyes, pushing them back into the skull, and if by chance the prisoner is still alive, they are left to die slowly."

Ruff looked shocked, almost wondering if this was indeed justice. It did not take long for the colonel to pick up on Ruff's disdain for this form of execution. "You must remember, old boy, these people are criminals, what sort of execution would it be if they did not suffer? They have caused suffering to someone, and now you say that they should be shown mercy, you would have to be pretty messed up to think that a criminal deserves a painless death."

Ruff looked as though he was starting to maybe understand. "I did hear, the death sentence exists for rape as well," said Ruff. The colonel looked at Ruff again.

"The bible says an eye for an eye and a tooth for a tooth, so the punishment must fit the crime," said the colonel. "There was a girl raped in Moontown a couple of years back, she was very young, but the defence jury tried to claim the person was mental and did not know what he was doing."

"Was he?" said Ruff.

"As it turns out, he was using it to get off," said the colonel.

"How so?" said Ruff.

"If you truly are mental, then you are locked away for life, and you never see the light of day," said the colonel.

"So, what happened when they found he was not mental?" said Ruff.

"They gave him the full penalty," said the colonel.

"Which is?" said Ruff.

The colonel looked straight at Ruff with a malevolent smile spreading across his face. "They tied down the blighter buck naked to a chair so he cannot move, and the straps are tested to make sure he cannot move. Then the executioner takes the offending appendage in her hand until it reaches the maximum size, then it is slowly cut away from the body, and the prisoner is left to bleed to death. Then the relatives are invited to watch the person die slowly. Believe me when I talk as someone who has experience of this sort of thing," said the colonel.

Ruff looked at the colonel as his expression had now changed. "I don't understand, love," said Ruff.

The colonel turned around to face Ruff with tears welling in his eyes. "The girl was my daughter. The pleasure I got watching him bleed slowly to death as his screams pierced the night, and the feeling as the silence hit the air, and the satisfaction of knowing that he died in abject agony was as close to justice as I could have hoped for," said the colonel.

"I have to ask, what is the crime rate in Moontown?" said Ruff.

"Very low, old boy. Why do you think this blighter has gone to all this trouble to hide his crimes? If it wasn't for you, we probably would never have identified him," said the colonel. Ruff looked impressed.

"Come on, love, let's find this book," said Ruff. The two men searched the library for what seemed like an eternity until finally the colonel said stop, he knew it was too much. "What's the matter, love?" said Ruff.

"You said yourself, old boy, we need to know what we are looking for. Any of these books could be the one we want, but without reading them all, how do we even know if it is here or not?" said the colonel.

Ruff thought for a moment then the mist started to clear. "This is probably beyond obvious, but what about a hunting book? Have you never heard the saying: people seldom look for what is under their nose?" said Ruff.

"Even so, old boy, I have to say, I think you're reaching." The two men followed the signs leading to the books on hunting until eventually they came across 10 books.

"Well, this shouldn't take too long," said Ruff. The colonel never answered. "What's wrong?"

The colonel stood just slightly back from the shelf with a tatty brown book in his hand, opened about halfway. Inside was a tape recorder; the book had been deliberately hollowed out to hold the tape. Ruff put forward his hand and, as gently as he could, he prized the book from the well and started to walk toward the tables to sit down.

The two men sat down both looked very nervous. "You realise that this could reveal everything we need to know, old boy," said the colonel.

"That thought had occurred to me, love," said Ruff.

The big man, still shaking, finally pressed down on the metal button, hoping he would hear Evelyn talking beyond the grave but instead, silence. The colonel gestured to Ruff, and Ruff handed the tape player to him. The colonel opened the holder, only to find that the reason for the silence was that someone had taken the tape. "Charles must have it, old boy," said the colonel.

"He must have realised that it was too obvious," said Ruff.

"So where is it?" asked the colonel.

Ruff pondered for a moment before finally speaking. "If the tape exists, I would guess he still has it in his possession," said Ruff.

"You don't think he would destroy the blighter do you, old boy?" said the colonel.

Ruff looked the old man up and down. How can you be diplomatic? he thought. "I hate to say it, Colonel, but if he does destroy the tape, what does he have to lose? In fact, if I am honest, he may gain a lot," said Ruff.

"So, you think he has destroyed it?" said the colonel.

Ruff again looked at him. "To be honest, no, no, I don't. I don't want to sound like some grizzled 1980s cop with the corny one-liners, but I think he will hold the tape as a bargaining chip," said Ruff.

"A bargaining chip, old boy?" came back the colonel.

"Yes, love, a bargaining chip. You may not believe this, but some things have a price far higher than money." The colonel looked like if he had a phone, Ruff would be in a rubber room now bouncing off the walls.

"Everyone needs money, old boy?" said the colonel.

"Even Charles?" came back Ruff. The colonel stroked his chin.

"No, old boy, not him," said the colonel straightforwardly.

"So, what do you do with money if you do not need it?"

Again, the colonel returned to his *I'm deep in thought* position. "I suppose there are charities."

"Did Charles have a favourite charity?" said Ruff.

"Charity, old boy? Charles was a cocktail party man; he was always at cocktail parties celebrating one thing or another. That was one thing with Charles, he did not need an excuse to party, if you told him there was a party, you can be rest assured he would find it," said the colonel.

"So, he did not donate to charities?" repeated Ruff.

"Charity begins and ends at home, old boy; if Charles had a charity, it was himself," said the colonel.

"So how did Charles become so wealthy?" asked Ruff.

"Rich parents, old boy, only child, parents die, you inherit the lot," said the colonel.

"By the lot, I take it we are talking millions, love?" said Ruff.

"Millions, billions, who knows? I know it was a lot, I was a close friend of the family, I knew his parents well," said the colonel.

"What were his parents like?" asked Ruff.

The colonel thought for a moment. "Michael was an industrialist, made his money in stocks and shares, but like a lot of rich people, you can never have enough money."

"His mother?" said Ruff.

"Cynthia did not like him, she resented him. You see, old boy, when one has a great deal of, how shall we say, social outlets and social lubrication, the one thing we cannot buy is what most want."

"That being love," said Ruff.

"Eternal life," said the colonel. "You think about it, you have so much money you know even if you gave it away, you would have enough to last 10 lifetimes. What is the one problem?" said the colonel.

Ruff thought for a moment. "I give in."

"Finding time to spend it, old boy," said the colonel. "I mean he can buy women, which is indeed a great skill." Ruff looked at him.

"I don't think prostitution is a good skill, love," said Ruff.

"I'm not talking prostitution, my dear boy, and besides which, prostitution is also punishable by death," said the colonel.

"Prostitution is one of the oldest professions in the world," said Ruff.

"In Moontown, it is immoral, old boy. If you're caught with your Christopher hanging out, you had better be going to the lavatory unless the lady happens to be your wife or girlfriend. What I am talking about is buying women. You see, old boy, Charles had so much money, he just had to open his wallet, and the women flocked to him, and he had a way with words, he could talk women into bed. Most women, if you whipped out your money and said, I want to buy you for the night, they would slap you or at least try to sweeten the offer, but Charles, they just said yes."

"What about the women, did they—?"

"Sample his merchandise? I did not know he was involved in drugs, old boy, and until you explained it all, I would never have thought it. But knowing Charles as I do, I doubt it, I do not think he would want a string of doped-up drug ladies, it would reflect badly on his image. You have to remember, until we catch him, only me and you know all this."

"Yes, it is quite something," came a voice as Ruff and the colonel spun round. When they finally turned, there he was, Charles Clearwater, the murderer.

"Charles, I guess you are going to tell us both how wrong Ruff is," said the colonel. Just then a pause, not a sound was heard in the library.

"I would love to, my dear Colonel Buttocks, but I am afraid what Ruff says is correct; I do manufacture drugs albeit with help from my lab technicians," said Charles.

"You committed the murders?" said the colonel.

Charles reached into his pocket, pulling out a pistol. "Yes, my dear colonel. I have a saying: when you're rich, you want more and more, but those people got in my way, so they had to have their lives ended. Believe me, it was the only way I could be sure they did not say anything. All my beautiful babies being infected with thrips, I could have cried, but I got my own back," said Charles.

"How?" asked Ruff.

"The tinctures were mine; I have some basic medical knowledge, and with a bit of help, I managed to cook up something, crude but nonetheless lethal," said Charles.

"The tape," said Ruff.

"Yes, you were right, you may be a building worker, but I realised after I had done it, someone would guess and find it, so I pulled out the tape," said Charles.

"I guess you are going to kill us now," said the colonel.

"Certainly. But if you think I am going to reveal everything I have done or where the lab is hidden, you are mistaken. This isn't some cheap movie where the baddie reveals everything he has done, then the goodie overcomes him to destroy the baddie's ill-gotten gains. No, I am sorry, but to err on the side of caution, all of that information stays with me," said Charles.

Charles walked away from Ruff and the colonel as he pulled back the hammer of the gun. "I think two head-shots will suffice, just in case you happen to be wearing bulletproof vests." Charles took aim and was about to shoot when he heard a noise. "What was that?" he asked.

"Sorry, love; that was me, I just dropped my pen. I know you're going to kill us, but can I pick it up before you do it?" said Ruff.

"Why?" asked Charles.

"Sentimental, love. When I started doing building work, the old lady I worked for underestimated my prices and she could not afford to pay. Poor old dear was in her eighties.

What can you do? I couldn't pursue her through the courts, so I pretended it was not a lot of work and I let her off, so as a thank you, she gave me a pen," said Ruff.

Still pointing the gun straight at the face of Ruff, Charles spoke. "OK, but very slowly," said Charles.

Ruff turned around so he could see where he had dropped it. Eventually, after much searching, he found it. "Here it is, love," said Ruff.

Ruff turned and slowly bent down. The jeans barely covering his more than ample cleavage slowly rolled down, revealing a lot more than was necessary, causing Charles to start gagging and choking causing him to drop the gun. This was the opening the colonel needed, he ran forward and without warning his hand flew forward and he picked up the gun. Without warning, his hand flew forward and, quick as a flash, he fired two shots straight into Charles. The bullets found their mark as his lifeless body slumped to the ground.

The door suddenly burst open and, in the door, stood two police officers along with Lady Pottersby. "What's going on, m'lady?" said the colonel.

"I was so worried about you and Ruff. I know I do not like people in my house, but the three of us have become so close. I was afraid you were in danger, so I called the police," said Lady Pottersby.

"It's a good job she did, what's the meaning of shooting people, sir?"

The colonel walked over to the lifeless body of Charles lying on the ground. Slowly, he opened his jacket and felt in the pocket, removing the tape before handing it to the officer. "This man is Charles Clearwater, and somewhere in these grounds, you will find a marijuana laboratory and, I daresay, also cocaine. Unfortunately, we have not been able to locate it yet, but the tape explains it all," said the colonel.

The officer looked at the colonel. If this evidence is on the tape, congratulations are in order, but tell me, how did you discover all this?" said the officer.

"Yes, Colonel, how did you know?" said Lady Pottersby.

"The answer to that lies with this man here. By day, a building worker, on the weekends, he attends murder mysteries, and if it had not been for him, I would say we would be no further on. May I present Ruff the Detective."

THE END

Lightning Source UK Ltd.
Milton Keynes UK
UKHW010618041220
374560UK00002B/235

9 781839 753008